THE Stud NEXT DOOR

New York Times & *USA Today* Bestselling Author

KENDALL RYAN

The Stud Next Door
Copyright © 2021 Kendall Ryan

Developmental Editing by
Rachel Brookes

Copy Editing by
Pam Berehulke

Cover Design and Formatting by
Uplifting Author Services

About the Book

Life threw me a curveball. An adorable eight-pound, four-ounce curveball with her mother's eyes and my dark hair. I'd like to think my single-dad game is strong, but honestly? I've been struggling a little.

When a beautiful young woman moves in next door and offers to give me a hand, I jump at the chance to hire her as a nanny. Jessa is amazing with my daughter. She's also patient, kind, and way too pretty.

The number one rule of hiring a nanny? Don't bed the nanny.

It's a rule I intend to keep.

But as the days pass, I begin to realize how much my life is missing. Companionship. Romance. Intimacy. When I discover my heart has space for one more female, it's a lost cause, another curveball. The hot-as-hell nanny is leaving soon for a mission trip to Central America. No sense in letting myself fantasize about Jessa being a permanent part of my life.

The closer we get, the more difficult it becomes to keep my feelings in check, because my heart won't listen. And neither will my libido.

Well, you know what they say. Rules are meant to be broken . . .

One

CONNOR

Sunlight pours onto the front porch of the three-bedroom home I bought several months ago. I gave up my apartment in the city for a suburban zip code, a lawn I don't have time to mow, and nosy neighbors who want to know why my baby's mom isn't in the picture.

It's . . . a lot.

But at this moment, lawn mowers and property taxes are the least of my concerns.

The stress I've been under for the last few months, ever since before my daughter was born, has been beaten into temporary submission by warm sunshine, good company, and the cold beer in my hand. Anxiety still lurks just below the surface, in the tension in my shoulders, in the dark thoughts that linger, but for now at least, I'm relatively at ease. Summer has finally come to Chicago, and I'm parked in a lawn chair on my front porch with three of my best friends.

"Just like old times. Right, man?" Hayes leans back in his chair, kicking his feet up onto the brick ledge. He's the easygoing one, always able to put people at ease.

I used to be that way. Friendly. Fun-loving. Always down for a good time. Now it's a mixed bag. The stress of becoming a single father has done a number on me, and I'm still fighting for breath on what feels like a sinking ship at times.

"Something like that," I murmur, lifting the bottle to my lips for a sip. The beer goes down with a bite, hoppy and full-bodied.

To my left, Wolfie grunts his approval. In contrast to Hayes, Wolfie is a bit of a handful. Complicated, but loyal. Unpredictably moody, yet reliable. Although his foul moods have improved drastically since he started dating my younger sister—a story that I have no intention of getting into right now.

"Thanks for the beer, man," I say, raising my beverage in Caleb's direction.

"Fuck yeah. Anytime," he says before downing what I can only assume is half of his beer and releasing an enormous belch.

Caleb is a bit of a wild child. I keep waiting for the guy to grow up, but so far, that hasn't happened. He's still the same shamelessly immature guy I met in college, and by all indications, that's not changing anytime soon.

"Chill, man," Hayes whispers to Caleb, nodding in my direction. "Boys' night isn't just for the *boys* anymore."

Ah. That's my cue to acknowledge the tiny little cherub resting in my arms. Marley, my baby girl, who has my dark hair and my ex's blue eyes and creamy skin.

"Oh, come on. She's dead asleep." Caleb leans forward in his chair. "Hey, Marley. Maaarley. Marzipan!"

My two-month-old daughter doesn't wake, nestled peacefully against my chest, her plump little fist clutching my T-shirt.

We all take a moment to watch the rise and fall of her back, the cutest little poop-and-puke machine you ever did see. Even when she's pooping and puking, she's the most beautiful thing in the world, and you can fight me on that. I'll die on that hill.

"How's she been?" Wolfie asks with a deep line etched between his brows, tipping his chin toward the sleeping baby.

I smile. I've missed my old roommate's perpetual frown.

Paternity leave has been . . . interesting. A bit isolating, but I'm starting to realize it doesn't have to be that way.

"Good. She's good." It isn't a lie. Marley is a good baby, usually low maintenance with only the occasional meltdown. Kind of like her dad.

"How about you?" Hayes frowns as he studies me.

Damn, I must look as exhausted as I feel.

"I'm alive." I chuckle, but the humor in my voice sounds forced. That's a new one for me.

"You'll feel better once you're back." Caleb nods sagely, as if my returning to work will somehow restore the balance of the universe.

"*If* I come back," I say to remind them, only half joking.

My partners graciously gave me six weeks of paid paternity leave, with a little leeway in the budget to sneak in another week or two.

Together, the guys and I own a sex toy business named Frisky Business, both an ecofriendly line of toys that we manufacture, as well as a retail store in the heart of Chicago. Despite the shop being a second home to me for years, I haven't set foot in the place in six weeks, and part of me can't picture myself going back. At least, not until I find someone I trust to take care of the most important person in my life, Marley.

"What about the day cares you were researching?" Wolfie asks, and I can see him crunching the numbers in his head.

I'm well aware that Frisky Business can't afford to keep me on paternity leave for much longer. It's already been two months.

I scowl. "No luck. Did you know there's a government website where you can look up safety violations and infractions of any licensed day care? It's terrifying," I say with a shudder that's all too real. "All the day cares within a five-mile radius have too many accident reports to even count."

"Shit, seriously? Well, what about Beth?" Hayes asks.

Ah, yes. Beth. Part-time mother of my child, full-time med-school student alongside her med-school-student boyfriend.

They certainly don't have the time to care for a child 24/7. We share joint custody, but a lot has been falling on me lately, not that I'm complaining. I love spending time with Marley, and I want Beth to be able to build her career. She's a good mom, juggling school, a new relationship, and Marley with relative ease.

"When she finishes her residency next year, she'll have more time to care for Marley. For now, she and Brett have her two days of the week. Beth wants more, but she can't quite swing it right now."

The guys nod, trying to understand this new life I've found myself living.

One day at a time . . .

Let's rewind. Thirteen months ago, I was happily single, living in the city without a care in the world. The only unknown in my life was the familiar and somewhat amusing panic of waking up next to a woman whose name I couldn't remember. Back then, I was going on a minimum of three dates per week, some of which ended with a satisfying hookup with whichever lucky lady could keep up with me.

My love-for-life dial was cranked up to 100 and locked into place with superglue. Nothing was gonna slow me down.

Of course, all that changed with a phone call from my former friend-with-benefits. Beth was busy becoming a doctor, and neither of us had time for a relationship. But Netflix and chilling became our thing for a couple of months last year, until those two little pink lines changed everything. Beth was carrying my baby, despite the precautions we'd taken.

But even with the massive overhaul of my social life, life is better with Marley, on all counts. She's given me purpose, a word I thought was only reserved for the kind of people who go on mission trips to Guatemala twice a year.

Nowadays, I'm so much more than just Connor Blake, the bachelor. More than co-owner of Chicago's number one sex-toy shop.

I'm a dad.

When I come to, I realize I've been droning on about day cares for give or take ten minutes. Even Wolfie's sharp eyes are starting to glaze over.

"In summary," I mutter, "finding a good day care in this neighborhood is a bitch."

"Why don't you just get a nanny?" Caleb says, cracking open his second beer. "I had the best nanny growing up. She still comes to my family's Christmas party each year."

"Probably 'cause you still need supervision." I

sneer at him, relishing the opportunity to give him a hard time.

But before Caleb can get a word out, Hayes cuts in.

"Where do you even find a nanny?"

"I'm sure there are databases for nannies," Wolfie says, ever the pragmatic one.

"I don't want to pick some random person off the internet, guys. If I get a nanny, they'd be alone in my home for the majority of the day. I'd need to trust them."

"Do you have anything valuable to steal?"

It's Caleb's turn to give me shit, and damn, does it feel like we're back in the shop. With a sleeping baby on my chest, I can't smack him upside the head like I normally would. I'll make up for it by teaching Marley to kick Uncle Caleb in the shins every chance she gets.

Hayes chuckles, shaking his head. "Other than his kid?"

Never too proud for a pissing contest, I'm about to tell him exactly how much I paid for my high-end espresso machine when a small sedan filled with moving boxes rolls to a halt in front of my neighbors' house. Mr. and Mrs. Wilkes have lived in that house for over two decades as happily re-tired empty nesters. I've only met them a couple of times, but the old couple have grown on me.

Hayes, Wolfie, and Caleb must sense my curi-osity, because the conversation stills as we wait to see who steps out of the car.

I hear the door slam and the soft padding of feet before I know who they belong to. When the driver comes into view to lift the roll-up door, I can't help but do a double-take because the girl is unbeliev-ably gorgeous.

She's young, around our age, with thick brown hair pulled back in a long, unruly ponytail. Wear-ing sneakers, shorts, and a loose-fitting T-shirt, she looks like any twenty-something on moving day. She opens the trunk and lifts out a hefty suitcase, clearly stronger than she looks, and sets it on the sidewalk.

"Do your neighbors have a hot daughter?" Ca-leb asks, standing to get a better look.

"Will you sit down?" Wolfie sighs, aging with every second that Caleb does anything immature.

For the first time in a while, I'm kind of with Caleb on this one. I'm curious.

"Just sons, as far as I know," I murmur.

When she reappears, I see her face for the first time. She's flushed, but not just with the summer heat. *She's excited.* And excitement looks really damn good on her.

"Jessa!"

We all turn to see Mr. and Mrs. Wilkes waving to her from their porch with wide, friendly smiles.

The woman we now know as Jessa sets a box down on the edge of the trunk and gives the old couple a wave. She jogs over to them, giving Mr. Wilkes a hearty handshake and Mrs. Wilkes a quick hug. I can't hear their conversation, but I get the impression they're meeting for the first time.

"All right, I'm bored." Caleb sighs, plopping back down in his chair. "Anyone want another beer? Or am I supposed to finish this twelve-pack all by myself?"

I peer down at Marley, who is squirming unhappily, her bleary little eyes opening and closing. I guess nap time is over.

Out of the corner of my eye, I see Jessa's box tilting over the lip of the trunk, about to topple. Instinctively, I jump to my feet, jostling the already grumpy baby. The box falls, Marley wails, Jessa and the Wilkeses turn, and suddenly everyone's eyes are on me.

"Fuck," I mutter under my breath. "It's okay, Marley. It's okay." I pat her back softly, but it's like comforting a fire alarm. I turn to the guys. "Would someone go help her with that box?"

Caleb and Wolfie spring into action as Hayes leans across the brick ledge with an apologetic smile for the neighbors. "Sorry for the commotion, folks. Can we help you out?"

"Oh, that's all right. It wasn't fragile stuff. Don't worry about it," Jessa calls back, her voice clear and cordial.

But Caleb and Wolfie have already rescued that box and are now unpacking the car, which contains a few more boxes, another suitcase, a smaller bag, and a duffel bag.

"Really, it's okay," she says, trying to intercept Wolfie on his trajectory to the Wilkeses' front porch. One look at him in the zone, and Jessa steps aside, her eyes wide and a timid smile on her lips. "Well, thanks, um . . ."

"Wolfie's the scary one. That idiot's Caleb," Hayes says, waving off her concern. "Best to just let them do their thing. They've already got an assembly line going."

And they do. Caleb stands near the car, pulling out boxes as Wolfie carries them an outside staircase that leads to a separate entrance on the second floor that Mr. and Mrs. Wilkes directed him to.

You'd better believe that I'd be right there with them if I didn't have a screaming baby in my arms. Marley's eyes are scrunched tightly closed, tears trailing down her pink cheeks.

I try rocking her. I try bouncing her.

Is she crying because she's tired? Hungry? Scared? I never fucking know.

In the ear that isn't already deaf, I hear Hayes making polite conversation.

"That's my buddy Connor's house." He points in my direction. "He's the normal one. I'm Hayes, by the way. Where are you coming from?"

"Oh, I'm Jessa. Nice to meet you. I'm from a couple hours east of here. Well, east is the lake. Southeast. I'm from Indiana." She laughs, somehow pulling off awkward and sweet at the same time.

Unable to take my eyes off of her, I ask, "What brings you to Chicago?" Instantly, I regret drawing attention to myself.

Yes, let's all look at the sad son of a bitch who has no idea how to calm his distraught baby.

I shift Marley's weight in my arms, hoping a new position will help. It doesn't.

I don't even hear Jessa's answer to my question, as much as I'd like to. While Jessa and Hayes make small talk as Wolfie and Caleb continue to unpack the trunk, I pace back and forth, trying to soothe Marley by gently patting her back and humming softly. I wish I knew what was wrong so I could fix it. She does this once in a while, and I've yet to figure it out.

"How old is she?"

I turn to see Jessa walking up the steps, a warm smile on her lips. She's close enough now that I can fully take in her features—light blue eyes, long lashes, and dozens of pretty freckles dotting her nose and cheeks. *The neighbor girl is cute as hell.*

"Uh, two months," I say, my tone harsher than I'd like it to be. *Why the fuck am I nervous?*

"The best months." Jessa nods, clasping her hands in front of her heart.

There's something so warm about this girl. It's like it comes off her in waves. I have to step back to keep from sweating. But she follows me, her arms outstretched.

What the . . .

"May I?" she asks softly.

My gaze darts to Hayes, who offers me nothing but a useless shrug.

"Uh, sure," I mutter, allowing Jessa to step into the same square footage as me. The smell of her is intoxicating, sweet and floral, a mixture of shampoo and something decidedly feminine.

Her hands brush against my arms as she scoops Marley into hers. My heart nearly stops when she flips Marley over, my dad brain warning me of danger. But when Jessa starts massaging Marley's back, the baby stops crying immediately.

"Gas bubbles," Jessa says, all smiles, and Marley sighs happily.

I'm damn near shocked speechless.

"Holy baby whisperer," Hayes blurts, his eyes wide.

I'm glad to see I'm not the only one blown away.

"How did you do that?" I ask, aware of how dumb I sound, but I don't even care. She's amazing.

"I'm the oldest of six. I can just tell," she says, her nose scrunching up adorably in unison with her shrug. "She should be settled now."

Humble too? Be still my cold, dead heart.

"Are you free for a nannying job?" Hayes asks, looking more at me than Jessa. "One that starts immediately."

I shoot him a glare and he glares back, his eyes saying, *What? You need a nanny, dude, and she's perfect.*

"Oh," she says with a laugh, her cheeks turning pink. "I don't know. I've never been a nanny before."

She carefully adjusts Marley so that she's supported comfortably. An unfamiliar warmth floods through my chest at the sight of my baby girl in Jessa's careful embrace.

"I guess I do need a part-time job," she says, more to herself than to me. "What's her name?"

"Marley," I say, hardly recognizing my own voice.

"Marley." Jessa coos, nuzzling her nose against my daughter's soft hair. "The perfect name for a perfect little girl."

Hayes cuts in. "And he's Connor, the dad. Could you give him your number?"

He means well, but this recruitment is downright aggressive. And annoying as hell.

Shaking my head, I say, "Please excuse my pushy ass of a friend. You don't have to—"

"No, I don't mind. I'll put it in your phone. Trade you."

With a moment's hesitation, I pull out my phone, and Jessa and I swap baby and device with minimal fumbling.

As her quick fingers type her number into my phone, her thumb ring catches my eye. It's delicate and feminine, a simple band wrapped around a small amber jewel. Did her boyfriend give that to her?

"Here you go. Nice to meet you, Connor," she murmurs, her long eyelashes casting shadows on her rosy cheeks. When she gives my phone back to me, our fingers brush with an electric shock.

"Sorry," she says. "Static electricity."

"All good." I chuckle, smiling sincerely for the first time in weeks. *Nice to meet you too, Jessa.*

As the sun begins its descent, Jessa and the Wilkeses head into the house. Marley is fast asleep in the crook of my arm. The guys are finishing off their final beers for the evening, and I'm utterly exhausted.

"Hire that girl," Hayes says firmly, clapping me on the shoulder. "You don't have to do it all by yourself. You need the help."

"Come on," I say with a scoff. "You heard her. She has no experience."

He shrugs. "Well, she knew how to get Marley to stop crying. She seemed pretty experienced to me."

I release a slow sigh. "I'll think about it. Now, get out of here so I can put Marley down for the night."

"Let's leave the man alone," Wolfie says quickly. He can always sense when it's time to leave, which is one of the things I love about him.

The guys say their good-byes, and before I know it, I'm alone again. Just me and my baby girl.

I miss having Wolfie as a roommate more than I'd like to admit, but we're both better off this way. No need to have both of us losing sleep at night, effectively knocking down Frisky Business's production levels by half. Besides, the man's in love, and with my sister, no less. Our friendship needed some space.

After kicking off my shoes, I heat up some leftovers and carry my plate and Marley into the living room. After I settle the baby into her body pillow on the couch beside me, I grab my dinner and the remote.

This is my favorite part of the day. I've worked hard to get Marley on a schedule. I know that I'll have to adjust it as she gets older, but for now, she crashes by seven, so this quiet time we get together before bed is pretty sweet. As I eat, she blinks up at me and listens to my predictions about Chicago's hockey team this season.

"Nystrom's looking good this year," I say, glancing at her. "I wonder if you'll be a hockey fan like your old man."

She stretches her arms over her head and lets out a yawn. I chuckle and take another bite of my food.

I hope we can share quiet moments like this as she grows. Eating pizza. Watching the game. Maybe even a little trash-talking about the opposing team. The idea of a precocious teenager with Beth's blue eyes and my dark hair sharing in some smack talk about any team who's *not* Chicago brings a smile to my face. I never imagined myself as a dad before, but now I can't imagine not having Marley in my life.

By the time I've finished eating, Marley's already asleep.

I carry her to her bedroom where her crib and changing station live. I've become something of an expert in changing diapers quickly and without any fuss.

Marley is still sound asleep when I lay her down on the soft mattress pad of her crib. In these moments, I don't feel like an actor performing the role of father. I *am* her father.

I watch her sleep, all soft sighs and tiny grasping fingers. *I love this little girl so damn much.*

The soft look on Jessa's face when she held Marley flashes through my thoughts. It was almost like she loved Marley too. Like she was her own.

I shake off the thought, recognizing it for what it is—my dad brain desperately looking for a mate to help rear my child. But even I know it wouldn't be healthy to fixate on the cute neighbor who settled my baby one time.

Talk about delusional.

As attracted as I am to Jessa, I can't let my imagination get the better of me. Even so, I can admire her bright blue eyes and distinct freckles. I can fantasize about her full lips, how they might feel under my fingers, under my own lips.

She's beautiful, and if I weren't emotionally unavailable, I wouldn't have questioned pursuing her. I would have pursued and kept pursuing until she was in my bed. But the reality is that I can't afford any distractions right now. Not when a tiny life depends on my full attention.

You need the help.

Hayes may have had a point. I can't stay holed up in my house as a full-time dad forever. I have to take breaks, I have to have fun, and most importantly—I have to get back to work.

Sitting on the edge of my bed, I tap out a text before I can psych myself out.

> If you're interested in that nanny position, let's talk. Would you be free for a chat tomorrow?

I press SEND. The message is direct and professional, with no indication of exactly how much I'm attracted to Jessa. And if I have any control over my libido, she'll never know.

Two

JESSA

This is *not* how I expected my summer to go. You couldn't even make this up if you tried.

The day I move into my new place, the perfect job practically falls into my lap? It's like a dream. Or a fantasy. Maybe I should check and make sure I'm not passed out on the side of the road somewhere in Wicker Park.

And it all happened so easily.

The stud next door needs a nanny. As the oldest of six, I know a thing or two about babies. Sure, I might not have direct experience, but my mom always had her hands full, and when there are that many little ones running around, you learn to start taking care of each other.

Besides, the man didn't know about gas bubbles, so I'm thinking I've got something to offer. He needs help, and I'm more than happy to provide him that service. Especially if that means I get to stare a little longer into those dreamy green eyes.

Connor Blake. Oh yeah, he's dreamy, all right. Who has a name like that in real life?

I couldn't get a read on whether he actually wanted to hire me or not, but his friends seemed so encouraging about the idea, that either way, he went with it. Watching the adorable baby next door would certainly be a sweet gig, not to mention that the commute would be ideal. Stumbling next door in yoga pants? Sign me up.

When we texted last night, Connor seemed a little stiff and short, communicating in brief phrases and one-word responses, but he agreed to have me over today. Whether that means this is an interview or if I have the job, I'm not quite sure. But I've got my fingers crossed, and my toes for good measure.

Because, let's be honest—I wasn't looking forward to applying and interviewing for jobs while trying to explain that I'm preparing to move to Central America in a few months. That doesn't exactly scream, "Hire me now."

With a huff, I toss my phone onto the bed and

decide to get ready. This hair isn't going to tame itself. And showing up to my first day (or interview or whatever it is) with an unruly mane of frizzy curls isn't exactly the best way to start off on the right foot.

I breeze through my cute little living room, admiring my new setup. I spent all afternoon perfecting the placement of my macramé wall hanging over the pale blue velvet couch, and the retro lamp I found at a garage sale last weekend turned out to be the perfect fit.

And I was lucky to find this rental on such short notice. The fact that it's the upstairs of an older couple's house means that I don't have to put my name on anything, I just hand them the money and peace out when my time comes. Not that that means I won't do my fair share of nesting in the meantime.

I check my appearance in the mirror, running my fingers through my curly long brown hair. I've kept my makeup light—just a little concealer and a few dabs of bronzer on the apples of my cheeks.

After slipping on a pair of shorts and a top I don't mind getting a little spit-up on, I take one last glance at myself in the mirror before heading out the door. The thought of Connor laying eyes on so much of my bare legs sends a little buzz of electricity down my spine.

Down, girl.

I never knew the single-dad thing could be so hot, but Connor is very attractive, dad or not.

I stuff my phone in my pocket, lock the door behind me, and take the less-than-a-minute walk from my door to Connor's. I can still feel the buzz of anticipation running along my spine as I wait for him to answer, and when the door opens, it transforms into a full-on zap.

Was his chest this broad and lickable yesterday? I wouldn't know—he wasn't wearing a gray T-shirt this fitted that hugs all his muscles.

His green eyes meet mine, and my insides liquify. I didn't know a person could *actually* have a dazzling smile. But there he is, Connor Blake, dazzling away at me with sweet baby Marley in his arms.

"Hey, Jessa, come on in."

It's hard not to swoon at the sound of his voice, warm and smooth like a scoop of vanilla ice cream melting on top of a freshly baked brownie.

All right, now I'm horny *and* hungry. *Focus, Jessa.*

"Thanks," I mumble, squeezing past him as he steps out of the doorway.

Baby Marley gurgles as I pass, and I smile and give her a little wave. She looks up at me, her big blue eyes shining with delight before she rests her face on her daddy's shoulder. It's so adorable, I'm about ready to die.

"Oh, you're being shy now? Because you were awfully chatty just a few minutes ago," Connor says, his voice light and playful as he talks to his daughter.

Okay, scratch that. *Now* it's so adorable I'm ready to die.

"Hi, Marley," I coo, waving again. "It's me, Jessa. Your neighbor."

Marley peers up at me from her daddy's chest, her lips parted in a sweet, gummy smile.

Connor grins. "I think she likes you."

I think she likes you too.

Talking about myself in the third person? Probably a sign that I'm not fit to watch his child. Thank God he can't hear what I'm thinking.

"Why don't we show you around," he says.

He shifts Marley onto his other side and leads

me through the entryway and into the living room, complete with a charcoal-gray accent wall, sleek built-in shelving, and a plush suede couch. It's homier than I imagined a bachelor pad would be— although I'm not sure it still counts as a bachelor pad if a two-month-old lives there as well.

"Obviously, this is the living room," he says, gesturing awkwardly.

I nod, realizing that I haven't said a word to the man since I set foot into his house, and manage to squeak out, "It's nice." *Smooth, Jessa.*

Connor nods and waves for me to follow him through the open-concept floor plan and into the kitchen.

"Formula's in the pantry. She breastfeeds when she's with her mom, but we've had a few miscommunications on pumping and passing on the milk lately. So it's back to keeping some formula in the house." He plants a kiss on the top of Marley's head, the look in his eyes somewhere between optimistic and frustrated.

"Has she been taking to the bottle okay?" It's not that I'm trying to pry, but if I'm going to help out around here, I need the full scoop. We'll get to Marley's mom in a minute.

He sighs. "Yes and no. She's been hit or miss

lately. I know she's hungry, but it's like she's picky or something."

"Well, you're warming the formula, right?"

Connor looks at me like I just spoke to him in Czech. "That's . . . something I'm supposed to be doing?"

"I mean, you don't *have* to, but if she's being finicky about the bottle, and she's used to the breast . . ."

He flashes me another one of his dazzling smiles. "See? This is why I need you. Desperately. *We* need you. I'm the idiot who serves his daughter cold formula. Please tell me you'll help us out. I'm willing to beg."

That string of short sentences makes me weak in the knees. So do his broad chest and white smile. Seriously, the guy is gorgeous.

"Of course. I would love to be Marley's nanny," I say, smiling and tucking my hair behind my ear.

"Thank God," he says on a relieved breath. Then he smiles widely at Marley. "Baby girl, Jessa is your new nanny. Actually, no, she's our lifesaver," he says brightly.

Marley gurgles in a way I'm deciding means she's happy, and Connor leads me upstairs for the rest of the tour.

"But I should tell you, I'm only available for the next two months. I have an assignment in Central America with a nonprofit organization all lined up then." I told him yesterday that I only needed something short-term, but it's best to be up front about things, I've found.

He nods. "Okay then. Two months. I'll take what I can get."

"So, does Marley see her mom often?" I ask, keeping my voice as casual as possible. Because it's not like I'm trying to ask about his love life. That's *not* what I'm interested in at all.

We enter Marley's bedroom, an adorable little nook painted pale pink. The crib linens, the rug in the center of the room, the curtains over the large bay window—all pink. Oh yeah, this guy totally went all out for his daughter.

"We're not together, if that's what you're asking," he says with a mischievous smile.

My cheeks flame. "Oh no, I was—"

"Nah, I'm just joking with you," Connor says quickly, his smile crinkling the corners of his eyes.

Not fair.

"We only dated for a couple of months before we got this little surprise," he says, nodding to Marley, who's currently drooling very happily onto his forearm. "Don't get me wrong—Marley's the best thing to ever happen to me. But it's not like her mom and I were planning on being together forever."

Point one for Jessa.

"We share custody. Marley stays with her mom a couple nights a week, and she's with me the rest of the time. It's all very amiable, but that's also why I only need the help part time. Between my kid and my business, there are a lot of balls to keep in the air." He chuckles a little at his own joke, and something tells me I'm missing out on the whole story.

"You own your own business?"

"Co-own. My buddies, who you had the unfortunate pleasure of meeting yesterday, and I own a sex-toy shop downtown . . . Frisky Business."

Jaw, meet floor.

Not only is this man hotter than hell and adorable with his baby girl, now he's well-versed in the bedroom too? As if it wasn't hard enough to keep myself from eye-fucking him throughout this whole home tour, now I have to live with the information that he owns a sex-toy store?

Good times.

Connor scans my face, watching for any sign of disapproval. Or maybe for signs of arousal? I don't know what he's looking for, but I know he's looking. And that's enough to send another buzz straight to my core.

Act normal, Jessa.

Breathe in. Breathe out.

"I might have to head downtown and check it out one day," I say, my body feeling like it's going to combust at any moment.

Connor licks his lips, and if I'm not mistaken, heat flashes through his eyes as he looks at me. "Tell me when, and I'll give you a grand tour of the store."

This is going to be a summer job unlike any other.

Three

CONNOR

"**A**re you kidding me with this thing?"

The electric-blue dildo hangs limply between two manicured fingers. It's held by my first customer of the day, a woman so disenchanted by what I assume is her first visit to a sex-toy shop that I actually feel sorry for her. Her face is set in a resolute frown, the toy held out with disgust in front of her, not unlike how I held my first dirty diaper.

"It's your favorite color," her boyfriend points out.

Isn't this how it always goes? One wants to try something new, but the other is resistant. One's looking for a little extra spice in the bedroom, but the other's a fan of the same old, same old. It's a matter of finding something that pleases both parties. Lucky for them, I specialize in toys for curious couples. By the time I'm done with these two, they'll be scampering back to bed to play with their new unmentionables.

"Sounds like you're looking for something a little more subtle," I murmur, rubbing my chin thoughtfully. *Damn, I'm overdue for a shave.* "I think I have just the thing. Come with me."

The couple follows me farther into the store. I haven't been here in almost two months, but these customers would never know the difference. I move through the displays with ease, pleased to find everything in its correct place. I let the couple peruse the shelves of discreet toys for a moment before I pluck a sample product off the shelf and pass it over.

"How about this? It's called the Joie De Vivre."

I hear Hayes snort from the front counter, trying to cover his laughter. The man knows my strategy. After the customers have explored on their own, sometimes laughing at the toys that verge on the cusp of garish, sometimes blushing with a bit of discomfort, I impress them with the sleek, expensive stuff. Works every time.

"What does it do?" the woman asks, her eyebrows raised.

I can tell by the way she's inspecting it that she's already a lot more comfortable with the size and shape of the thing. So I explain how the couple's toy works, beginning with the functionality of the device and ending with its special features— multiple vibration settings, 100 percent silicone design, waterproof exterior, discreet case.

But as I'm answering their questions, there's an unfamiliar emptiness in my voice. The customers are none the wiser, but it feels like I'm reading from a script. Before I became a dad, I used to take pride in helping couples with their sex lives. Now I just feel like a fraud.

My own sex life is nonexistent. My libido is next to gone, except in the inconvenient moments when it's appeared like a tornado around Jessa.

Not gonna lie . . . the girl inspires a whirlwind of conflicting emotions in me.

Jessa is a total pro when it comes to babies— anyone could see that. It honestly shocks me that she hasn't nannied before. She just seems to know things about babies, things that I haven't figured out in my two months of fatherhood. She makes it look easy. Too easy. But she's also very pretty, and that's been more than a little distracting.

My dad brain wants me to wife her, and my

dick wants me to bed her. The romantic in me wonders if I could do both, but then the businessman in me shuts it all down with the simple but cogent reminder: *She's the nanny. You're her employer. Don't be a creep.*

It goes on like this for the rest of the day as I help customers find the right fit for their needs, all the while doing my best not to think about using the very same products with Jessa. Wondering how her sweet voice would sound begging for more . . .

And just like that, I'm hard. *Fucking seriously?*

I tell Hayes a bald-face lie in mid-debrief, saying I have to piss, just so I can splash some cold water on my face and take a breather. *Keep it together, man.* I either need to jerk off tonight or switch professions.

That settles it. It's time to call it a day.

With that sobering thought, I exit the bathroom and call out to the guys, "I'm heading out."

Hayes glances at his watch, a slow smile spreading on his face. "You made it longer than I thought you would. Six whole hours."

I chuckle, grabbing my keys and wallet from my desk drawer. "You've got to ease into these things, I've found."

He gives me a short wave. "Glad you're back, dude. Makes a huge difference."

"It's good to be back."

Caleb pokes his head out of the stockroom, a cocky expression on his dumb face. "You know, we were fine without you, dickwad."

"Tell that to the books," I shoot back, feinting a punch inches from his nose.

He flinches and swears, knocking my fist away before returning to the stockroom with a grumble.

"Give Marley our love," Wolfie mumbles distractedly from his own workstation, his gaze glued to his computer.

I call over my shoulder, "You got it," and let the door swing closed behind me.

My commute back up Lake Shore Drive to the northern suburbs takes me a little less than a half hour, but I'm grateful for the time to think.

When Marley was born, it seemed like I would never have time to myself again. Being a single dad means life is busier than ever, while still feeling crushingly lonely. The thought of coming home to a woman—coming home to *Jessa*—sends a tingling warmth up my spine, all the way to my heart.

Whoa, there. Fantasizing about the nanny is unavoidable, but catching feelings? There's no way I'm going to let *that* happen.

It has to be because she's the first woman I've had in my home—well, other than my female friends, right? And because she's good for Marley? Yeah, that's got to be it. Definitely no catching feelings.

Be realistic, dude.

The lights are on in the kitchen when I pull into my driveway. My chest tightens at the sight of a woman's silhouette standing at the sink. I try to shake off the residual sentiment by taking the steps two at a time.

Before I turn the house key in the lock, I take a moment to steel myself. *Be cool.* With a sharp inhalation, I twist the knob.

Just as I do so, the door swings open, Jessa greeting me on the other side. Her cheeks are a rosy pink, and her hair is pulled back into a ponytail like the first time I met her. *She's just as beautiful.*

"I heard the car pull in. Thought I'd let you in," she says softly.

Marley is tucked against her chest in some sort of makeshift sling, fast asleep. The sight of her brings a smile to my lips.

Jessa turns on her heel to wave me indoors. "Welcome back."

"Thanks," I murmur, instantly distracted by the way her ass looks in that pair of heather-gray yoga pants. Two plump and perky handfuls.

Remember all that steely resolve? Yeah, it's just a puddle of pathetic mush now.

"How was she today?" I kick off my shoes, noticing an unfamiliar pair of red-orange sneakers tucked onto the mat next to my own black ones. *Cute.*

"We had a bit of a mess around lunchtime, but otherwise she was an angel."

I follow Jessa into the kitchen, and the scent of garlic fills my nostrils like I'm stepping into an Italian bistro. My stomach growls as I catch sight of steaming pasta and freshly cut vegetables.

"You made dinner?"

"Yeah, I hope you don't mind. I figured it's your first day back, so you'd probably be tired."

"That's really thoughtful of you," I say, a smile twitching at the corner of my mouth. "Smells great. What is it?"

"Pasta primavera, maybe." She chuckles, peeking over the lip of the small saucepan to monitor whatever buttery sauce she has going. "Mrs. Wilkes let me snag a few veggies from her garden. You'll have to let me know how it turns out."

I lean against the door frame, crossing my arms. "Why don't you stay for dinner?"

The wooden spoon stills in the pot. After a second, Jessa looks at me over her shoulder and shrugs. "Sure, why not?"

After transferring Marley from the sling into a portable bassinet since she's still sound asleep, we sit down to eat. The pasta is cooked to perfection, fragrant with fresh garden flavors. Warm food in my stomach and dry wine on my lips, I'm more relaxed in this moment than I've been in . . . well, months.

"This is really good," Jessa murmurs into her wineglass, indulging in another sip. "Tastes expensive."

"It's not. Just a grocery store brand." I laugh, enjoying the flush that creeps over her cheeks. Making Jessa blush may be my new favorite pastime.

"I wouldn't know." She smiles, shaking her head slightly. "I'm more of a beer gal."

All right. That's just not fighting fair.

"They have beer where you're going?" I ask, popping another forkful of pasta into my mouth. Not the smoothest transition, but I'm curious. I mean, why Central America?

"Don't they have beer everywhere?" she says, one eyebrow raised in challenge. Seems it's better to be direct with this woman.

"I should hope so. What will you be doing down there, anyway?"

"Well, the nonprofit helps folks in El Salvador prepare to emigrate to America. Assisting with documents, simulating naturalization interviews, and so on. I'm going to be working with the children, specifically."

My eyebrows raise of their own volition. "That's cool."

"Thanks." She smiles nonchalantly, my words rolling off her as easily as if I'd reminded her the sky is blue.

"Seriously, Jessa. You're really impressive. I can't say I know anyone else who has mission work on their résumé."

"Well, it's not on my résumé yet . . ."

"But it will be. Is this just like a one-time thing, or is it something you want to pursue?"

She smiles, poking at her pasta with her fork. "I've actually thought about becoming an immigration lawyer. But that would mean I'd have to go back to school."

Blown away, I lean back in my chair. The level of ambition at this table makes me feel like a hack. A deep laugh rumbles from my belly.

"What?" she asks, cocking her head to the side.

"Nothing. I just didn't know I was employing a superhero. But I guess I should have known, considering you did save my ass within minutes of meeting me."

"Oh, come on." She rolls her eyes, but her adorable grin is impossible to miss.

"In all seriousness . . ." I sigh, letting my gaze wander up to the ceiling. "I really respect that. What you're up to is a lot more admirable than selling vibrators and massage oil for a living."

"Don't say that," she says, her voice firm. "A healthy, active sex life is important too."

Our eyes lock. Suddenly, I don't know if we're just having small talk or if Jessa feels the same connection I do. A flurry of fantasies ricochet around in my head, like someone lit off a firework in there.

Just when I'm about to open my mouth and agree with her that sex is important, there's a knock at the door.

"Who's that?" Jessa asks, concern creasing her brow.

"I have no idea."

When I open the door, I'm surprised to find Maren and Scarlett on my front porch with wide, goofy smiles on their faces.

"Surprise," they both exclaim, lifting twin foil-wrapped casserole dishes into the air. Slung over their shoulders are large grocery bags filled to the brim with diapers and baby wipes.

"Hey." I chuckle, any moodiness melting away into appreciation. I'd forgotten Maren had promised to bring over supplies one of these days when she learned from Hayes that I'd been struggling. "Come on in."

The women pass me the casseroles unceremoniously, eager to see Marley, I'm sure. They follow me through the front hall, complimenting my new digs. But no surround sound system or new sectional could compare to the shock of finding a beautiful woman sitting in my dining room at a table that clearly screams *dinner for two*.

"Hi," Jessa says cheerfully. "I'm Jessa, the nanny."

"The nanny, huh?" Scarlett murmurs, turning to me with eyebrows waggling.

I narrow my eyes at her. *Don't even start.*

"I'm Maren, and this is Scarlett. It's wonderful to meet you. I've heard great things," Maren says, walking directly to Jessa with a hand outstretched.

"Already?" Jessa laughs.

They clasp hands warmly, exchanging genuine smiles.

"You made an excellent first impression," Maren says. "Something about being a baby wizard?"

Jessa shakes her head, smiling. "Oh, a whisperer."

"That was it!"

They both laugh. Leave it to Maren to become fast friends with Jessa.

"I'll put these in the fridge," I say, casseroles in hand as I make my way to the kitchen.

Working some Tetris magic, I manage to find

space in the fridge for both the casseroles and our dinner leftovers. I make a quick job of clearing the counters before securing a cork into the bottle of red Jessa liked so much and tucking it back in the wine rack.

When I reemerge from the kitchen, I clock some movement in Marley's bassinet. There she is, wide awake with big blue eyes blinking up at me.

With a smile, I lift my baby girl into my arms, cuddling her against my chest. She reaches for my shirt instinctively with one set of chubby fingers, the others finding their home in her gummy little mouth. Is it possible to love anything more than I love this girl?

The quiet, serene moment is interrupted by Scarlett, as it often is, who squeals at the sight of Marley in my arms. She rushes to my side, her face fixed in a look of complete and utter adoration.

"Oh my God, she's so fat. Has she always been this fat? Hi, baby." Scarlett reaches out to caress my daughter's chunky leg, and Marley gurgles with each ticklish touch.

"Thanks, Scarlett," I grumble, rolling my eyes. Now I have to worry about overfeeding my kid.

"That's totally normal," Jessa says quickly, reading my mind. "Some babies have extra fat storage for developmental purposes."

"I thought you said you were, and I quote, 'wildly unqualified for the job.'" Maren chuckles, one hand propped on her hip like a scolding schoolteacher. "Sounds like you know plenty."

Jessa shrugs, her smile humble and amused at the same time. "I owe it to Connor for giving me a chance."

"She acts like I wasn't the one begging for help," I say, arching one eyebrow. "Did she tell you about the bottle slash formula incident?"

"Oh God." Jessa giggles. "He didn't know you should warm a bottle before feeding the baby." She smiles, the faint freckles on her cheeks and nose growing more noticeable with the flush of her skin.

If only I could brush my lips against that smile . . .

"Uh-huh." Scarlett's fascinated gaze pings between us.

Maren laughs politely, always the one to recover from awkward situations first.

Fuck, I must look like some jackass, flirting with the nanny in front of my friends. But I'm not really flirting. Inside jokes aren't flirting, right?

"Well, we'd love to show you around the city—" Maren says, just as Scarlett jumps in.

"If Connor is willing to give you a night off." Scarlett cocks her head at me with a look that says, *You expect me to believe you aren't fucking the nanny?*

"I'd love that. I won't usually be here this late," Jessa says quickly, as if she's coming to my defense. "He just invited me to stay for dinner tonight."

"Oh, did he?" Scarlett sings, inspecting her nails.

Goddammit. Time to say good-night.

"It's getting late. I'd better get this one to sleep," I say gruffly, wishing Marley looked at all tired. Instead, she's wide-eyed and seems to be enjoying this just as much as Scarlett. "Thanks for bringing all the stuff by. I really appreciate it."

"Anytime. We'll let ourselves out," Maren says with a soft, apologetic smile.

I exchange hugs with the two women and Jessa follows them to the door, exchanging phone numbers and promises to connect soon. When I hear the front door click and Scarlett's car exit the driveway, Jessa returns. This time, she's wearing her red-orange sneakers and has her purse slung over her shoulder. I almost wish she didn't have to go.

"I'd better get going too. I'm sure you're exhausted after your first day back," she says softly, her fingers tensing and untensing around her purse strap.

My heart twinges with an unfamiliar pang. *I don't want Jessa to leave*. My mind races for reasons why she should stay . . . but I come up completely blank.

"I'll walk you out."

I follow Jessa out the front door and onto the porch where we stand for a moment, listening to the cicadas.

"It's a beautiful night," she murmurs, playing with the end of her ponytail as the wind teases her flyaways.

What I wouldn't give to tuck those curly strands behind her ear right now. Anything for the chance just to touch her.

Man, I'm really losing it.

"Yeah, it is," I finally reply.

Unexpectedly, Jessa takes two steps closer to me, leaning in. She plants a soft kiss on Marley's chubby cheek, a picture of peace and serenity—all the while my heart beats as loudly and wildly as the fireworks finale on the Fourth of July.

"See you tomorrow, baby girl," she whispers into my daughter's ear. Before she steps back, she looks up at me through her eyelashes. Our bodies are so close, I can feel us breathing in unison.

"See you tomorrow too." She smiles with lips so kissable, I have to look away before I make a fool of myself.

"See you," I manage to say, my voice hoarse.

With that, Jessa bounces down the stairs and cuts across the Wilkeses' lawn and up the stairs to the door of her new apartment—only a faint shadow in the streetlight when she turns back to wave good-bye.

When she's safely at home, I step inside my own door and close it slowly, pressing my forehead to the cool wooden frame. Marley squirms in my arms, her big eyes searching my face as if I alone hold the answers to life's greatest mysteries.

"I don't know, Marley girl," I murmur, pressing my lips to her soft head of hair. "Daddy has no idea what he's doing."

Four

JESSA

"Cheers, ladies. Here's to being young and beautiful in the Windy City."

My new friends—Penelope, Scarlett, and Maren—raise their wineglasses, each with a warm smile directed my way.

"And to our new friend, Jessa," Scarlett says, looking to me with a toss of her long auburn hair. "Welcome to the neighborhood, but more importantly, welcome to the whirlwind that is the men of Frisky Business." Her face holds a challenging smirk, and I'm not quite sure what to make of it.

Before we even clink glasses, Maren and Penelope are both balking. Maren's polite smile is frozen on her face, and Penelope winces uncomfortably.

Clearly, we've already ventured to the most exciting and controversial topic of the evening. And something tells me if I want to learn anything about Connor, Scarlett will be my go-to source.

But just as quickly as the topic was broached, the moment passes, and Maren and Penelope are back to their sweet and blissful selves. We sip our sauvignon blanc and drool over menu items before settling on the beef empanadas and goat cheese for the table.

I have to admit, when they first recommended a tapas place, I wasn't sure what to expect. But between the cool brick walls, the warm atmosphere, and fragrant tapas food coming from the kitchen, I'm sold.

"Okay, so remind me again how you all know each other?" I ask, placing my hands flat on the table and looking helplessly between my three new friends.

They're all so . . . pretty. Is it normal for friends to be this pretty? Scarlett's more on the eccentric side in a bright pink dress and chunky orange necklace. Maren's a little more on the demure side in an olive-green tank dress that hugs her curves and makes her hazel eyes pop. And Penelope is just too damn sweet in a baby-pink silk top and the kind of vintage jeans only models can pull off. I've got to know how these three very different women found each other.

Maren smiles. "Scarlett and I go way back," she says, turning to smile at her old friend. "We've been running this city forever."

"And I'm with Wolfie," Penelope says with a shy smile. "Maren's brother. But we were friends before that happened."

"*With* as in . . ." I let the question hang in the air between us. Part of me knows the answer, but I don't want to leave anything open for interpretation.

"In a relationship," Maren says with a smile, "and I'm so happy for you two. Besides, it's not like I'm one to talk."

"Wait, I'm lost. What does that mean?" I ask. My head's starting to spin, trying to keep up.

The three women laugh and Scarlett clears her throat, clasping her hands together in front of her chest. "This is what I meant when I said that the men of Frisky Business were a shit show."

"I think the term you used was *whirlwind*," Maren says, correcting her with a strained smile.

"Whatever. It's complicated. Let me explain." Scarlett takes another sip of her wine before continuing. "Okay, so your new boss, Connor, co-owns the sexy-times operation with Hayes, Wolfie, Caleb, and Ever. These two ladies are dating Hayes and Wolfie. Maren and Hayes dated in secret, but Hayes and Wolfie were best friends, and that was a problem because Wolfie is Maren's older brother. But now it's all happily ever after, and the moral of the story is that everyone is getting some dick except for me."

"Scarlett!"

Maren swats her arm while Penelope buries her face in her hands.

"What?" Scarlett says with an innocent look on her face. "True story. Anyway, now they're all coupled up, and it's mostly fine, except that Wolfie is Maren's brother and Penelope is Connor's baby sister. And, of course, all of these men co-own one of the most successful sex-toy shops in the city. No wonder they're so goddamn horny." She chuckles at her own joke.

I nod along slowly, trying not to let my eyes pop out of my head. Guess I'm not the only one who was a little more than interested in how unusual Connor's company was.

And I have to say, I'm more relieved than ever to have found this group of women. I was beginning to think that the situation I was in was too complicated for anyone else to understand. But complicated is what these girls know best. Maybe they can help me navigate the waters with Connor without me losing my head.

Scarlett continues, a sly smile curling on her lips. "And that brings us to you, Jessa. The new girl on the scene, and Connor's cute new nanny. What brings you to our neck of the woods?"

My heart leaps at the thought of being paired with Connor, even if it's only as his nanny. I've only known Scarlett for forty-eight hours, but I've been around her enough to know exactly what she's implying. Still, I breeze past the suggestive description and focus on introducing myself to my new friends. It'll be a long summer without some female companionship.

"I just needed a place to stay for the summer," I say with a shrug, "and the couple who live next to Connor was renting out the top floor. And then when I was moving in, Connor happened to have a crying baby, I happen to be one of six kids, and Hayes suggested I become Marley's nanny. It all just kind of . . . happened."

"Talk about good luck," Maren says whimsically.

"Or fate," Scarlett adds with a dip of her chin.

"Why just the summer?" Penelope asks.

I swirl the ruby-colored wine in my glass. "I'm leaving for a mission trip to Central America in August. I'll be gone for six months, and my lease was up in May."

I watch their eyes widen as I explain what I'll be doing and where I'll be going. I've almost gotten used to the half-awed, half-horror-stricken look people give me when I tell them. Yes, I'll be living in a third-world country, and no, this kind of work isn't for everyone. But it's also hard to come right out and tell someone that you think they're crazy for doing it.

Maren reaches across the table to give my hand a light squeeze. "That sounds amazing."

"Six months is a long time to be away," Penelope says. "Are you worried about getting homesick?"

I tilt my head, considering her question. "Yes and no. I'm excited about the opportunity and all the work we'll be doing. I know it'll be hard to be gone for so long, but it also helps to know it's not forever."

"You're an angel among heathens, that's for

sure," Scarlett says.

"Speak for yourself," Maren mutters.

"Baby Marley will miss you," Penelope says kindly. "And Connor will too. He's going to have his hands full without you."

Scarlett scowls. "It's not like she's the baby's mother. She's only a nanny, and she's free to do whatever she wants. Connor can find someone to replace her."

"I just meant that I'm sure Jessa will be very helpful to them," Penelope says meekly.

"I'm sure Connor will enjoy the process of searching for her replacement," Scarlett says with a suggestive waggle of her eyebrows.

Maren giggles, and Penelope cracks a sheepish smile.

"What does that mean?" I ask, trying to keep my tone as light and casual as possible—the exact opposite of how I'm feeling.

I'm dying for any shred of information about Connor, something beyond the tiny hints and sparks that have flared up between us. I have to know what his deal is. And even more than that, I have to know if he's into me. A hungry little ball of need forms deep in my belly every time I lay eyes on him, and something tells me it's not going away anytime soon.

Scarlett grins. "Penelope? Would you like to give our new friend a little history lesson on your brother?"

Penelope's small smile spreads into a smirk. "I thought we were having a girls' night, not a let's-talk-about-my-brother night," she says innocently.

"I just want to know a little bit more about the man I'm working for, that's all. He's not a serial killer or anything, right?" I ask, keeping my voice as deadpan as possible.

That gets a good laugh out of the group.

Penelope smiles, a slight wine flush on her cheeks. "Nah, Connor's a sweet guy, especially since Marley arrived. She's really changed him."

"You can say that again," Scarlett says with a snort, and Maren almost shoots wine out of her nose.

"Was he not sweet before?" I ask. Visions of a darker bad-boy version of Connor swirl through my mind. I'm not going to lie, I'm into it.

"Connor's always been sweet," Maren says with a pointed look at Scarlett. "He was just a bit of a playboy before the baby was born. Even before then, really. There wasn't anything romantic between him and Marley's mom, but he took good care of her. He went with her to all the doctor's appointments and birthing classes. He was just super involved and supportive."

"And he bought *everything*. Cribs, car seats, you name it. That baby became his whole life. He became a totally different person overnight. He grew up," Penelope says with a wistful look in her eye. "I'm super proud of him."

"He's risen to the challenge," Scarlett says reluctantly, "I'll give him that much. Sold his motorcycle. Stopped dating around. Got his priorities straight. I wasn't sure he had it in him."

I might not know her that well yet, but I can already tell it's high praise coming from Scarlett.

A brief silence falls over the table, but I feel a question rising in the back of my head, and I can't keep myself from asking it.

A crease forms in my brow. "So, when you say he was a playboy . . ."

The three women exchange weighted glances, but it's Scarlett who responds.

"Total manwhore."

My windpipe tightens, and I suppress my look

of shock.

I try to imagine an immature playboy version of Connor, one who would have taken one look at the young, single girl moving in next door and found a way into her pants that same night, but I can't picture it. I like this version of Connor. The responsible caretaker who does what's right for his daughter, who puts her needs before his own.

But let's be honest. In my imagination, this responsible version of Connor still finds his way into my pants. Okay, fine . . . I'd invite him in.

God, I have to get this under control. Just thinking about him makes me feel all hot and bothered.

I take a long gulp of wine to help cool myself down. It doesn't work, of course. Ever since I met him, my libido has been cranked in overdrive. It makes zero sense.

Penelope continues about her brother, a thoughtful look on her face. "What Connor really needs is a nice woman who's good with Marley. Someone who can match his level of responsibility, while also being able to handle the fact that he runs a sex-toy store."

"Might not be as hard as you think." Maren winks. "We're here, aren't we?"

"Hayes didn't have a two-month-old when you started dating."

Maren shrugs. "I'd like to think I could have handled it."

"Oh, please. You could barely handle the potential disapproval of your big brother," Scarlett says.

We all laugh, but I don't laugh quite as loudly as the other three.

Could I be that woman for Connor? I'm definitely good with Marley, and the chemistry between Connor and me is hard to deny. Images of the life we could have together scroll through my mind . . .

Connor and me feeding Marley in his kitchen. The three of us going for beach days by the lake. Connor and me stealing kisses in the front seat while Marley dozes in the back of the car. It could be so simple, so easy, so sweet.

Except for the fact that I won't be here in a few months.

Reality tears through my brain like a category five hurricane, obliterating any trace of the fantasy I'd just had.

I'm leaving the country, and that's that. No

more lake days, no more flirting with neighbors. I'll be thousands of miles away from here, helping people who look different from me and speak a different language. Connor and Marley will be distant memories—except there's a small part of me that worries they really won't be.

My attraction to Connor doesn't matter, despite how much it might be growing. I can't hurt him, and I can't hurt his daughter. I stuff my feelings away in the same dark place I put the fantasies, somewhere they won't resurface. Somewhere they'll wither away and let me get through this summer in peace.

If they don't, I don't know how I'll survive.

Five

CONNOR

"So, what do you think? It's too big, right?"

Hayes slides a new kind of sex toy across the desk in my direction. We're all gathered in the stockroom, huddled around the toy like a bunch of little kids looking at a bug. I take the device in my hand, raising my eyebrows at the heft of it.

Wolfie crosses his arms over his chest. "It might be too much for our usual crowd."

We're demoing the product for the week, deciding if we want to bring it on for good. It's a new brand for us, one we've never carried, and the product has some serious action-packed features.

"This conversation is interesting and all," Caleb says with a waggle of his eyebrows. "But we all know what needs to happen. One of us takes it home, gives it a go, and then reports back his findings."

"Well, it won't be me," I say with a grunt. This dad isn't going to be getting any action anytime soon.

Suddenly all eyes are on me, the guys' expressions varying from concerned to skeptical.

"What?" I grumble, silently cursing for drawing attention to myself.

A slow smile unfurls on Hayes' lips. "Usually you're the first to jump on a take-home demo."

I shrug. Yeah, maybe the old me. Things have changed this past year. How does he not recognize that?

The bell on the front door rings, and we all turn our heads. When I move to go and greet the customer, Hayes catches my shoulder. "Caleb, can you—"

"On it." Caleb gives Hayes a mock salute, hopping over some cardboard boxes on his way out.

Wolfie grunts, slides his laptop under his arm, and makes himself scarce.

"When was the last time you went on a date?"

Hayes asks in full-on intervention mode, his brows knitted in concern.

"I don't fucking know," I say with a sigh. I dated a few women after Beth, but the news of her pregnancy killed any chance of pursuing a second date. And God knows I haven't slept with anyone since.

"You good, man?" Hayes asks.

"Yeah. No. I'm fine," I say with a little laugh. But the sound that comes out of me is more of a strained cough than the good-natured chuckle it's meant to be. "It's been almost a year."

"Since . . ."

I lean in, keeping my voice low. I'm man enough not to be ashamed of it, but I definitely don't want to shout it from the rooftops. "It's been almost a year since I've had sex."

Hayes's eyes widen as the words hang limply in the air between us.

I'm about to come up with some lame-ass excuse about being a working dad when the door creaks and my attention swings in that direction. Caleb leans against the door frame, and behind him, Jessa stands like a statue with Marley in her stroller, squirming happily at the sight of me.

"What impeccable timing," Hayes says under his breath.

I'm off the hook, at least for now, about answering his questions. But based on his reaction, I can tell Hayes isn't going to let this go.

"Hi," Jessa says softly, her expression guarded.

I have no doubt that she overheard everything I just said. *Fuck.*

"Jessa, good to see you." Hayes jumps in, recovering quickly and finessing the situation like the pro he is. "Let's go, Caleb. We've got shit to do."

As he and Caleb leave us in the back room, I take a little comfort in the sight of him smacking Caleb upside the head on their way out.

I'd completely forgotten that Jessa said she was going to come by sometime this week. Being the genuinely kind human she is, she expressed interest. Then I, being the genuinely insane human that I am, told her to drop by Frisky Business with Marley whenever she wanted to.

Not like seeing Jessa around the very toys I've imagined demoing *with her* would fuck with my head at all. Not one bit.

I'm such a dumbass.

"Hey," I say, flashing her a grin that will hopefully erase all memory of what she just heard from the record.

She smiles back, the blush on her cheeks only growing pinker. *So much for that.*

"You guys having a good day?" I reach down to unlatch Marley from her stroller and ruffle her hair.

"We sure are." Jessa nods. "Had breakfast, then a nap. I figured we'd take a little outing before lunch."

"Sounds like it's been a great day so far." This kind of conversation I can do. Let's keep it to small talk, and I'm golden.

"What's that?" she asks, nodding toward the conspicuous toy still resting innocently on the desk.

And suddenly we've veered from business to personal very, very quickly. I set it down out of sight.

"Just a toy we're thinking about adding to our regular inventory," I say with a shrug, lifting Marley out of the stroller and into my arms. When I press a big fat kiss to her big fat cheek, I think I hear Jessa sigh. "You okay?"

"Oh yeah, I'm fine," she says a little loudly. Catching herself, she smiles. "It's just cute seeing you two together."

"Yeah?" I chuckle, trying to keep Marley's hands from venturing inside my mouth. "This is cute, huh?"

"Uh-huh." Jessa nods, meeting my eyes as she tucks a strand of hair behind her ear.

When our gaze locks for a second longer than what is deemed casual, she ducks her head and busies herself, looking down the aisles of the stockroom. So I take the opportunity to check her out.

Today, her hair is down, brushing the skin of her collarbones and shoulders, which would be bare if not for the thin straps of her dress. It's a soft, summery fabric with white and yellow flowers, and stops just above her knees. On her feet are the sneakers I've come to look forward to seeing on the front hall mat. A sexy but sensible outfit, like she wanted to impress me but knew she was still on the job. My dick strains against my zipper at the thought.

When she bends over a cardboard box to read the label, I catch the sight of black panties before I can force myself to look away. *Hot damn.*

"This place is a wreck right now. Want the grand tour?" I ask, gesturing to the door. The shop is bigger and has better air flow, and I'm counting on it to clear my head.

"Sure," she chirps, spinning around.

When she passes me, I can smell the floral scent of body lotion on her skin. Suddenly, I'm accosted with images of Jessa naked, fresh out of the shower and bending down to rub scented lotion over one long leg and then the other.

Since when have I turned into a teenager who can't stop thinking with his dick?

After handing Marley off to the guys for quality uncle time, Jessa and I spend almost an hour walking around the shop, making pleasant conversation. She has a lot of questions about the business itself, which I much prefer over the usual "What does this one do?" The less I have to explain the mechanics of sex toys to the nanny I want in my bed, the less likely I am to imagine using them with her. Well, at least not while she's right next to me.

A little while later, Jessa and Marley set off for home, and I finish the rest of the afternoon in a distracted state. Thankfully, Hayes doesn't ask any more questions about my love life, but I can tell they're on the tip of his tongue.

By the time I make it home late that afternoon, Marley's napping again, and Jessa is standing at the sink, wrapping up a couple of chores.

"She's sleeping again?" I ask, stepping into the kitchen.

Turning, Jessa gives me a warm smile. "Yup. I think our outing today tired her out."

"Really?"

Jessa nods. "But I think she liked seeing you during the middle of the day."

"Yeah, I'm glad you guys stopped by."

Neither of us says anything else for a long moment.

I normally enjoy a comfortable silence, but with today's events, I have to clear the air. But before I can say anything, the very words I'm thinking about come tumbling from Jessa's mouth.

"I just want to say that I'm really sorry about earlier," she says carefully, her voice concerned.

I glance over to find her turned toward me, examining my expression. Jessa looks so legitimately worried that I can't help the smile that breaks out across my face. "Sorry about what? You have nothing to be sorry for."

"I didn't mean to eavesdrop. Caleb led me to the back room, and when he opened the door—"

"Seriously, Jess. You have nothing to worry about. Caleb, on the other hand, got a minor beating from Hayes."

"Are you serious? I must have missed that." Jessa laughs, snorting a little.

She's so fucking cute.

I lean against the counter, relaxing a bit. "Yeah, so don't worry. It's all good."

See? That wasn't so hard. But when Jessa speaks again, my heart drops.

"I guess I just . . ."

Fuck, I guess we're not done with this conversation.

"It seems so unlikely. You're so attractive. And young and single. And you're a great dad." She states all of these compliments as facts, completely unaware of how they affect me. But her words do affect me—a slight buzz hums through me at the idea that Jessa finds me attractive, that she thinks I'm a great catch.

In my experience with women, I'm used to playful banter and the never-ending back-and-forth. It comes with the territory of having a little sister and several female friends. I don't know how to handle someone who gives out compliments like candy on Halloween.

"Thank you," I murmur, grateful to see that Jessa's focus is back on the bottles and nipples she's arranging on a drying rack on my kitchen counter, and not on my awkward fucking face. Because I don't know whether to smile or play it cool.

"I mean it," she says solemnly. "You're a total catch."

Am I fucking blushing? Jesus Christ, Connor, pull yourself together. A cute girl gives you a compliment and you're red in the face? Is this middle school?

"I don't know about that." I duck my head to rub the back of my neck, hoping she'll let up on the deluge of affirmations.

Don't get me wrong, I like them and all. It's just making it hard to respond like a normal human. I was serious when I told Hayes it had been a minute.

"Oh, come on." Jessa scoffs, turning toward me again, her expression serious. "If you ever wanted to go on a date," she says, and my heart clenches, "and need me to watch Marley for the night, just let me know."

My heart sinks. *She's not fucking interested, man. Get it through your thick skull.*

"No, I'm good," I grunt out, coming off more curt than I mean to.

I guess this shit is getting to me. It's a bracing thought, but it's true.

If I dated, I'd only want to go on a date *with Jessa*. I'd take her out to a nice dinner, maybe a late-night walk by the lake.

But I know there's only two ways this could go. She's into it, and suddenly I'm employing my girlfriend who will be leaving for six months. It would be sticky, and confusing, not ideal for a healthy relationship. Or she isn't into it, and it's so awkward that she quits and I'm stuck looking for a nanny again. Neither is a very good option.

"Okay," she says softly, probably sensing she's hit a nerve.

I desperately want to tell Jessa that I'm only bothered because, at this point, I'm into *her*. Not anyone else.

But I know in my gut that it's better to just let things lie.

Six

JESSA

With my arms full of bags of groceries, I begin the trudge from my car up to my second-floor apartment. It's funny—it didn't seem like that far of a journey when I decided I could carry a week's worth of groceries all in one trip. But judging by the ache in my shoulders and the amount of plastic already cutting into my wrists, I think I might have misjudged this one.

Nice going, Jessa. Great choices all around.

Connor's deep voice carries from his doorway just as I'm about to take my first steps up the stairwell. "Hey, neighbor, need a hand with those?"

A nervous knot forms inside my stomach at the sight of him, as gorgeous as ever in a pair of black athletic shorts riding low on his trim hips, and a light gray T-shirt that looks soft enough to bury my face into. Or maybe I just want to bury my face into his pecs.

"That would be great, thanks," I manage to squeak out, trying to adjust my grip on an especially heavy bag of fruit and yogurt.

In a few long strides, Connor is by my side, our fingers brushing as I hand him a few bags. My stomach dips with every brief moment of contact. God, it's really hard to focus on anything other than him when he's around.

"How's Marley?" I blurt as we climb the stairs to my apartment.

There's something unsettling about knowing his face is ass-level. Is he the kind of man to do the gentlemanly thing and look away, even if he knows I can't see him? Or is he totally sneaking a glance at my butt right now?

"She's with her mom, probably sleeping or eating. Blissfully unaware of what the real world is like." Connor's voice is flat and monotone, a far cry from his usual warm and engaging baritone.

"You okay?" I ask, turning the key to my little side entrance. I'm grateful for my own access point to this apartment. The couple who own this place have done a great job making it feel like an independent property.

As we place the bags on the counter, he lets out a sigh. He looks around before answering, taking my space in.

It's not until this moment that I realize Connor Blake is standing in my kitchen. I invited him in without thinking twice about it. I didn't even pause to make sure there weren't old takeout boxes piled on top of the trash can, which thankfully there aren't.

He rests one hand on the counter and leans into it. "I'm supposed to go out of town tomorrow on business for an overnight, but I'm picking Marley up this evening and she doesn't go back to her mom's until next week. I know it sounds like a small thing to be so worked up about, but it's just . . ." He trails off, staring at the counter.

"I get it," I say, taking a step toward him. "I can stay over and watch Marley for you, if you want. So you can go and don't have to worry about her."

Connor shakes his head, his gaze still trained on the counter. "No, I'm planning on canceling. I don't want to miss out on any of the time I have with Marley. She's growing so fast."

Is it possible for a heart to actually melt a little bit? Because I think that mine might be dripping into a puddle on the floor.

"I'll go with you then." The words come out before I can fully think them through. Apparently, this is becoming a consistent problem when I'm around Connor.

He looks up at me then, his green eyes making my heart beat double-time. "I can't ask you to do that."

"You're not. I'm offering. Take me with you. I'll babysit Marley while you're off doing whatever sex-related dealings you have to do," I say with a smirk.

I expect Connor to laugh or at least crack a smile at my joke about his business, but he doesn't. Instead, his brow furrows and his eyes grow more serious. He's thinking. Deeply. About what, I have no idea.

It's a win-win for him. He can do his business and also see his daughter. What is there to think about?

After a beat of silence, during which I'm ready to hide from the embarrassment of inviting myself on his trip, his expression changes and his emerald eyes lock with mine again.

"Okay." Connor nods, a small smile spreading on his lips.

"Okay, as in yes, you'll take me with you?"

"Okay, as in I'd be grateful to have you come with us and watch Marley while I work. I'll put you up in a hotel room, of course. Everything will be covered, and you'll get a fantastic bonus too."

A thrill runs along my spine at the thought of a night away. "So, where are we going?"

"Indianapolis," he says, pulling his phone out of his pocket. "Shit, I've got to run, but I'll text you the details, okay?" He pauses and meets my eyes again. "Thank you, seriously, for saving me with this. I really don't know what I'd do without you."

I nod and shrug at the same time, so overwhelmed that I probably look more like I'm having a tiny muscle spasm. But I don't care. Because I'm going on a trip with my hot neighbor and his adorable little girl, and no amount of awkwardness on my part can stop it.

As promised, Connor texts me the details shortly after he heads back to his place. I spend the rest of my day organizing my little kitchenette and planning out my outfits for our one-night stay.

It's a lot of pressure trying to figure out what to wear that strikes the perfect balance between "I find you incredibly sexy" and "I'm still fit to take care of your two-month-old child." But I'd like to think I've picked out some options that find that sweet spot.

The next morning, I meet Connor and baby Marley out by his car at eight a.m. sharp, just as he requested. I'm not sure what I was expecting, but one look at Connor nearly gives me heart palpitations.

I'm used to casual Connor, or even business-casual Connor, but this? In a crisp pair of navy-blue slacks and a white button-down with the sleeves rolled up halfway? This is business-meeting Connor, and I really freaking like what I see.

Who knew I was so into forearms? And when he bends over to secure Marley into her car seat? Yeah, let's just say those slacks hug him in all the right places.

The drive from Chicago to Indianapolis isn't too bad. We alternate between listening to Connor's music and chatting about his job, both of which are opportunities for me to stop obsessing about every little thing that's happening.

By the time we arrive at the hotel, Connor still has a solid hour before his meetings begin. He heads into the lobby to check us in while I tend to a fussy Marley, who's more than ready to be freed from her car seat. I unbuckle the straps and pull her out into my arms, bouncing and rocking her while holding her to my chest. She's warm and a little sweaty, like most babies after a nap, but the sweet smell of her skin brings a smile to my face.

All things considered, she's a little angel baby. I have no problem hanging out with her in my room today. In fact, it might be difficult to give her back to Connor tonight.

I turn to the sound of footsteps approaching behind me. It's Connor, with some papers from the hotel in his hand and a grimace on his face.

"What's wrong?" I ask. There's no reason to beat around the bush anymore. It's obvious when something's up with him.

He squints uncomfortably, looking down at the asphalt. "It's the reservation."

"Was there a problem? Do we need to find somewhere else to stay?"

"Uh . . . well, no. There was a mix-up."

"A mix-up?"

"They gave us one room."

"Oh."

"With a king-size bed."

"*Oh.*"

"The one thing they can accommodate is a baby. They'll be bringing a crib up for Marley shortly."

My mind starts reeling faster than I can catch up with it. One room. King-size bed. Connor and me, sleeping in it together. Tonight. Right now. It's happening.

Holy shit.

"Jessa, I'm sorry, this is so inappropriate." He groans, scrubbing a hand roughly over his face.

I snap out of my horny dreamland and plaster a polite, sympathetic smile on my face. "Hey, don't worry about it. It's not your fault. A king-size bed is practically a small island. I'm sure we can make it through one night unscathed, right?"

My words come out cool and casual, but I'm not sure if either of us believes them.

Connor's expression is an unreadable mask. If I didn't know better, I would think he's mad about something.

After a slow inhale, he turns and takes our bags out of the trunk and then leads the way up to the room. *Our* room. The room where we'll be sharing a bed tonight. My body buzzes with anticipation, and I squeeze my fingernails into my palm to try to fight it.

He's right. These thoughts—these little moments of excitement—are beyond inappropriate. Connor is my boss, even if I'm just the nanny to his baby daughter. If I'm going to make it through this stay with both my dignity and my summer job intact, I'm going to have to find a way to quell these fantasies. And fast.

The room is pretty standard for any business-class hotel. Neutral-patterned carpeting, beige-paneled walls, a dark chestnut desk in the corner with a small minifridge wedged underneath it.

What stands out more than anything is the bed.

For the first time in my life, a king doesn't look quite as massive as I remember. The plush white comforter and a pile of decorative pillows almost look like a challenge: *Not as innocent as we seem, huh?* As promised, a crib has been brought up and placed at the foot of the bed, leaving just enough room for Connor to squeeze by and set his stuff by the desk.

I stand awkwardly on the other side of the room where he left me, a sleepy Marley curled up against my chest. He avoids my eyes as he bustles around the room, making a few last-minute preparations before leaving for his meeting.

"She should be ready for a nap shortly after I leave," he says absentmindedly, scrolling through his phone and abruptly stuffing it in his pocket. "I should be back late this afternoon. I figure we can order in, and then watch a movie or something?"

He still can't meet my eyes when he says it, but I can't help noticing how much that suggestion sounds like a date. Or it would if I weren't here for the express purpose of babysitting his daughter.

"Sounds good to me. I'm easy."

Connor seems to catch the double entendre before I do, pausing in midstride on his brisk walk out the door. My cheeks burn with embarrassment.

Can this situation get any more uncomfortable?

But he lets it go, turning to give me a curt nod before closing the door behind him. No matter how embarrassed I might have felt just moments ago, I'm already looking forward to his return.

My day of watching Marley goes by quickly. She goes down for her nap like a champ, and is sweet and happy when she wakes back up. We watch a little TV, I let her babble and feed her when she's hungry, and before I know it, Connor's texting me asking what I want for dinner.

We order delivery from a Mexican restaurant

nearby, and turn on some made-for-TV movie that has us both crying with laughter because of how ridiculous the plot twists are. Sure, it's not exactly how I imagined I'd be spending my evening, but I have to say it isn't half bad.

Connor is easy to be around. Even though I'm very attracted to him, he's kept his distance, and I know he'll respect my boundaries.

Later, he puts Marley down for the night while I change and get ready for bed in the bathroom. My heart pounds while I brush my teeth, scrubbing my tongue a little harder than usual. If I'm about to share a bed with Connor Blake, there's no way I'm going to bed with salsa breath.

I walk out of the bathroom to find him sitting on the edge of the bed in a worn T-shirt and boxers, and my heart just about jumps out of my throat. Suddenly, my silk sleep shorts and oversized shirt make me feel self-conscious in front of him, and not nearly as sexy or confident as I'd hoped. Not that I ever thought he and I would be sharing a room, let alone climbing into the same bed together.

"Are you done in there?" he asks, barely meeting my eyes.

"Mm-hmm," I squeak back, skirting around him and fishing my phone charger out of my bag.

The sooner I can find something to do with my hands, the sooner I can stop thinking about how badly I need to not be looking at his crotch.

But *holy shit*, those black boxer briefs really hugged him in places I would like to explore. I realize he probably didn't pack any pajamas because he assumed he'd have his own room.

Taking a deep breath, I force my mind out of the gutter. I can hear the sink running as Connor brushes his teeth, and I climb under the covers on my side of the bed, careful not to disturb his side too much. It's not like there's clear etiquette on how to go about handling sharing a bed with the father of the child you're nannying, who also happens to be a sexy Greek god of a human being. But I think giving him his space and being respectful of it is a good place to start.

I'm scrolling through my phone, pretending I'm reading something very important, when Connor comes back out of the bathroom and joins me in bed. The mattress shifts to accommodate his weight, and a fresh batch of goose bumps crop up on my skin at the thought of how close we are right now.

So many things can happen under the covers. So many things that no one would ever have to know about. So many things I've dreamed about in my sleep.

"Thanks again for coming with us." His voice is low and sincere, and it cuts straight through me.

"You're welcome," I manage to say, even though my throat is suddenly dry.

"Good night, Jessa. Sleep well."

Hearing my name on his lips sends a shiver down my spine, and that same ball of need winds itself tighter in my gut.

"You too."

In the morning, I wake curled up on my side, feeling warm and secure, more comfortable and well-rested than I've been in a long time.

With my eyes still closed, I stretch out one of my legs, and it brushes against something firm—firmer than a pillow or a comforter would be. I stretch my leg further, almost beginning to straighten out, when I feel something warm and firm behind me, and then something heavy across my side and over my chest.

The haziness of sleep slowly slips away from my brain, and I realize what's happening.

It's Connor. I'm cuddling with Connor. Or rather, Connor's cuddling me. He's pressed against my backside, spooning me in his sleep.

Suddenly, I'm completely awake, but I'm not about to do anything to stop what's happening yet. His breathing is still deep and slow, which means he's still asleep, which means I get to savor this for a few moments longer.

The feel of his strong arm draped over my waist, his broad, muscular chest pressing into my back, the scent of his aftershave—it's all a rush. It doesn't take long until I'm aware of how accessible my most sensitive parts are to his hands. How easy it would be for this position to become something more.

He stirs, taking in a deep breath and flexing his biceps against me. I sigh and stretch too, pretending like I'm waking up as well. I turn just in time for Connor to groggily open his eyes. When he realizes where he is—what we're doing—he pulls away, and I instinctually mirror his movements.

"Shit," he says, his voice raspy with sleep. "Sorry."

"No, it's fine. But I'm sorry too. This is awkward."

Why do I always babble so much when I'm

around him? Why can't I be as cool and smooth as he is in situations like this?

Connor doesn't respond, merely grunts in response.

It's probably too early to have a full-on conversation about this. But still, for the rest of the morning, I can't get the feel of his arms around me out of my head. Or his scent. Or the image of how sexy he looks in nothing but a T-shirt and a pair of boxers.

Even if nothing ever happens between us, something tells me I'll be thinking about last night for a long time.

Seven

CONNOR

"**B**irthday shots, birthday shots!"

With four shot glasses crammed haphazardly between his fingers, Caleb approaches our pool table with a goofy smile on his face. Judging by the color of the liquor, or lack thereof, it's either tequila or vodka. No limes, though, so either Caleb half-assed the order or he's entirely forgotten how much I hate vodka. Either could be true.

Despite his egging on, Hayes and Wolfie kindly don't join in on the ridiculous chant. Caleb distributes each glass before holding his aloft, the rest of us following suit.

"Here's to another dirty thirty, my man. Cheers!"

If I sighed any deeper, I might deflate entirely.

Yes, it's my birthday, and yes, I know I should be living it up, celebrating with my friends, and I am—I'm here. But my brain is still back at home, a big part of me wishing I was chilling on my couch with my little girl and the sports highlights on TV.

As of tonight, I'm no longer a twenty-something with nothing but time to lose. Now I'm a thirty-year-old single dad who feels out of place in smelly bars with shitty pool tables. Don't get me wrong, I'm grateful my friends got me out of the house tonight. It was overdue. And with Jessa at home, it's nice knowing Marley is fine without me every now and then.

With Caleb on a mission that can only end with us suffering from hangovers tomorrow, I'm sensing there's an expectation that I'll let loose like I used to. To them, Crazy Connor isn't such a distant memory. But to me, those days feel like a lifetime ago.

We toss back our shots, and I shudder from the sharp, acetonic flavor of cheap vodka. *Jesus. That's nasty.*

"You couldn't have gotten the good stuff?" Wolfie grumbles, quickly chasing the bitterness away with a gulp of some dark imperial stout.

"Look, I asked for middle-shelf. There's a strategy to this. Start with the nasty shit, then slowly move on to the good shit—it makes it harder to quit. And it makes it so, so much easier to get our birthday boy wasted."

"One, that's backward as hell. Two, I'm not here to get drunk," I say grumpily, lifting my glass of ice water as proof. "Marley's at home with the nanny, and I don't want to come home smelling like cheap vodka."

"The *nanny*." Hayes chuckles to himself, raising his pint glass to his smirking mouth.

"The *hot* nanny," Caleb says, punctuating his unnecessary addition with a belch.

Classy.

Even Wolfie smirks, one eyebrow crooked. "Like we all don't already know her name."

"Okay, fine," I say with a shrug. "Marley is at home with *Jessa*."

"Oh, Jessa. Riiight, Jessa." Caleb smacks his palm to his forehead in a mock eureka moment. "I forgot her name, 'cause you didn't mention her in the last, I dunno, five minutes."

"Shut up," I grumble.

I get it. They all think it's hilarious that I haven't fucked the insanely attractive nanny. I only bring her up a lot because she's taking care of my daughter, and these dickwads wouldn't understand the relationship between a parent and his child's caretaker. It's crystal clear to me, as long as I ignore the burning desire I feel for her every time we're in the same vicinity.

"You're one to talk, Caleb." Hayes juts his chin toward Wolfie. "We were just talking about you and Scarlett."

Caleb freezes with his shot glass in midair. "What about her? What about us?"

"It just seems like your friendship has . . . what was the word you used?"

Hayes nudges Wolfie, who very matter-of-factly grunts out, "Evolved."

"No, it hasn't." Caleb scoffs, swearing as the cue ball drops into the pocket.

I didn't see this turn of conversation coming, but I'm suddenly very interested. And frankly grateful the focus isn't on me anymore.

"I always thought she had a thing for you," I say, leaning over the corner of the table to clap him hard on the arm. I snicker when he scowls at me.

"No, man, it's not like that. Scarlett and I are strictly friends."

"Of course." Hayes nods solemnly. "Well, let me remind you that I'm Maren's confidant, who happens to be Scarlett's confidante, and word travels—"

"I'm getting more shots," Caleb says quickly, tossing his pool cue to me before turning on his heel and storming back to the bar.

I glance at Hayes and Wolfie, and the three of us exchange a knowing look. *Let's drop it.*

I check my watch reflexively, noting the time. I've already been out for a couple of hours. It would be best if we wrapped this up soon so I can get home and relieve Jessa of her babysitting duties.

"Thinking about the nanny?" Wolfie asks, leaning against the pool table while Hayes takes his shot.

I'd bristle at the question, but coming from Wolfie, I know there's no subtext behind it.

"Yeah, I guess I am," I say with a sigh. "I feel bad staying out late while she's waiting for me at home."

Hayes makes a face, pursing his lips as if to stop whatever he's thinking from tumbling out of his mouth.

Son of a bitch.

I give him a challenging look. "Whatever you're thinking, just say it."

Caleb returns with more shots, for once reading the damn room and keeping his mouth shut.

"That just sounds like something I'd say about Maren," Hayes says, giving me a knowing look.

"And I'd say about Penelope," Wolfie adds.

I scrunch my eyes closed and run a hand through my hair. *When will my friends just leave well enough alone?* "That doesn't mean anything."

"You'd tell us if there was something going on, right?" Hayes asks, his brow furrowed.

What a bunch of gossips.

"There's nothing to tell."

Absolutely nothing. Certainly not the fact that we slept in the same bed the other night, and I woke up curled around her soft, sweet curves. Definitely not how I contemplated for just a moment about pressing a kiss to the back of her neck and grinding my raging hard-on against her ass, desperate to take this *thing* we have to the next level.

"We talking 'bout the hot nanny again?" Caleb whispers conspiratorially, passing shot glasses to Hayes and Wolfie before holding one out to me.

"Man, I said I was done drinking." I groan, shaking my head.

"You never explicitly said that." Caleb shrugs, nodding toward the shot glass in his outstretched hand.

All eyes are on me as they wait for me to do one of two things—either admit that I'm into the nanny, or down this shot. And God knows I'm not about to confess my dirty little secret just yet.

I grab the glass from Caleb's hand and throw back the shot in one painful gulp. They all watch silently, waiting for me to recover from the taste of literal gasoline.

I raise a single finger, my voice hoarse as I croak out, "One more, two at most."

Caleb hoots in triumph while Wolfie and Hayes exchange a fist bump.

Sorry, Jessa. Looks like it's gonna be a long night after all.

By my fifth shot, I'm officially drunk. My tolerance is at an all-time low, thanks to months of only drinking the occasional beer or glass of wine.

After arranging our rideshares, Hayes shares a car with me, which is more of an effort on his part to make sure my drunk ass makes it safely to my front door. I struggle to stay vertical during the car ride. When our driver pulls up to my house, I pull myself upright.

"That was fast," I mumble, smoothing my hair back with one hand.

Damn, I even smell like I'm drunk. A real class act, Connor.

"You knocked out for a bit there." Hayes chuckles, his gaze trained on his phone. He's probably texting Maren all about my reckless night of drinking. "Need me to get you inside? Dismiss 'the nanny'?"

I shoot him a lazy glare and open my door. "I got it. Thanks."

"See you tomorrow, bud."

I shut the car door, swaying a little as I watch the headlights disappear down the road.

It takes me roughly ten years, but I manage to unlock the front door, kick off my shoes, and wander to the kitchen. Leaning against the fridge, I force myself to drink two full glasses of water. Since stumbling through the door, I've made some noise, so it strikes me as strange that Jessa hasn't poked her head in here yet.

Something could be wrong, though I sincerely hope not. Maybe she just fell asleep? It is pretty late.

The lights in the hall are dark. Marley's nursery is dark too, except for the single star-shaped night-light on the shelf. I tiptoe into her room and gaze down into the crib.

Marley's sleeping peacefully, all warm and cozy in her little monkey onesie. She's so fucking cute that I have to shove down the urge to scoop her into my arms and press a kiss to her cheek. But I leave her be, knowing it's not worth waking her up and spending the rest of the night comforting a grumpy baby.

The guest room across the hall is also dark, the bed untouched. I know Jessa would never leave Marley alone and just go home . . . so the question is, where the hell is she? It's then that I notice my bedroom door is slightly cracked open, a sliver of light cast onto the hallway carpet.

As I give it a gentle push, the door opens silently. And there she is, curled up on my bed, her limbs tangled in my favorite gray cotton blanket.

A soft-cover book rests on Jessa's chest, rising and falling with each slow breath. In the lamplight, her eyelashes cast dark shadows across her freckled cheeks, and all those gorgeous mahogany curls spill over my white pillows.

I don't know how long I stand there like a creep, staring at her, but I know I could watch her for hours. She's beautiful like this, with all the formalities and professionalism forgotten. Even more beautiful because she's *in my bed*.

I try to be as quiet as I can, softly padding across the floor to kneel next to the bed.

Damn. She looks so peaceful. I really don't want to wake her. But even my inebriated brain knows that I have to.

When I caress the back of her hand with my fingertips, Jessa blinks awake, her eyes heavy with sleep. The smile that sprawls across her warm, rosy lips is so easy and trusting that it makes my chest tighten.

"Hey there," she murmurs, tilting her head to get a better look at me.

"Hey," I say softly, smiling genuinely for the

first time all night.

She chuckles. "Sorry for stealing your bed." Her voice is raspy with sleep and, if you ask me, sexy as hell. "I thought I'd hear Marley if she woke up since you share a wall. Didn't mean to fall asleep."

"That's okay."

She props herself up on one elbow and drags her fingers through her bed head. The strap of her tank top hangs loosely on her shoulder, and it's harder than usual to wrench my gaze away. I watch as two fingers tuck under the strap, lifting it back to its rightful place, only to remain on her shoulder and caress the sleep-warmed skin there.

Fuck. Those are *my* fingers, not hers.

"Thank you," she whispers, the words falling from her lips like melted butter as her blue eyes search my face for something like clarity.

You won't find that there, Jessa. All you'll find is a tormented man, telling himself to take his damn hand away.

But I don't. And she doesn't pull away. Instead, she leans into the touch, and now my whole palm rests on her arm, my thumb rubbing circles against the freckles dotting her shoulder.

"Did you have a good time tonight?" she asks, biting her lip in a way that has me leaning into her against all logic.

"Yeah." I struggle to pull in a breath, my gaze hooked on that hypnotizing mouth of hers. "Did you?"

She smiles. "Yes, it was fine."

"That's good," I whisper.

I should ask Jessa something about how my daughter did, or if she went to bed okay . . . but all I can do is keep staring at her mouth.

The words hang in the air for less than a second before I take a chance and close the distance between us. Jessa's breath hitches, and I feel her hand grab at the front of my shirt, pulling me in.

And just like that, we're locked together in a breathless kiss. Her book falls to the floor with a faint thud, no match for the pounding of my heart in my ears.

Her lips are warm and so unbelievably soft against mine, opening to my tongue with an eagerness that I feel right against my pants zipper. My hand slides up her neck to tangle in her hair, tilting her head to deepen our kiss and eliciting a whimper from deep in her throat. Her moans are sweeter than a goddamn daiquiri, and I'm drunk on the taste of her—

Oh my God. I'm drunk.

Ashamed, I pull away, our lips parting with a wet pop. My hand drops from her curls to clench the sheets between us. My eyes closed, I take a few slow breaths.

Jessa unknots her hand from my shirt and whispers, "Are you okay?" The concern in her voice is almost heartbreaking.

"Yeah, I'm fine," I manage to choke out. "I'm drunk. I'm sorry. I don't know why I did that."

"It's okay," she says softly, reassuring me.

She runs a hand through my hair, which does nothing to calm the tension in my jeans. Throwing off the blankets, she scoots off my bed and grabs her book from the floor.

"I'd better get going. Happy birthday, Connor. I hope this year is the best one yet."

She pads away, her footsteps growing quieter until I hear the faint latch of the front door. I stand up too quickly, my head swimming for the moment it takes me to ground myself in the present.

I just made out with Marley's nanny. I just

made out with *Jessa.* And it felt incredible.

Fuck, fuck, fuck.

Eight

JESSA

"Hey, Scar, remind me again where you want this box to go?" Maren calls out from down the hallway.

Scarlett's mouth screws up to one side while she thinks, scanning the room. "Um . . ."

A small smile forms on my face. "Any day now, Scar. These boxes aren't exactly as light as a feather."

Scarlett shrugs. "Sorry, I don't know. Just drop it in here, and we'll figure it out together."

Maren huffs loudly and grunts her way into the living room to join us, setting the box down with a loud thud. She wipes the sweat from her forehead with the back of her hand and glares at Scarlett.

"Next time, if you're going to be indecisive,

you can carry the box full of old trashy tabloids. Why are you lugging those things around with you, anyway?"

Scarlett ignores Maren's little jab and continues organizing flatware in the kitchen.

Maren looks at me, her eyes wide, and I get the message. *Can you believe her?* she's trying to tell me, but I know better than to get between old friends. Especially old friends who are getting testy because of the stress of moving. And quite possibly hangry too.

But I'm about to move several thousand miles away, so I know a thing or two about that particular kind of stress.

"I'm hungry. Are you guys hungry?" I ask, keeping my tone light and chipper so it's not obvious I'm trying to distract them.

"Starving." Scarlett groans and throws herself across the olive velvet couch.

"I could eat." Maren picks at a stray thread fraying the hem of her shorts as she agrees.

"So, what are we thinking? Chinese? Thai? Mexican? Pizza? I saw a place around the corner that looked pretty good."

Both of their faces light up at my last suggestion.

Maren's stomach growls, and she places her hands over her belly, a look of surprise sneaking across her face. "Okay, maybe I'm hungrier than I thought."

"That pizza place is the bomb," Scarlett says. "My old place isn't far from here, and I've eaten there many times."

I pull up the pizzeria's menu on my phone and start scrolling. My mouth waters just reading the topping options. Moving's harder work than you realize, even if you pay a couple of burly men to do most of the heavy lifting for you.

"You wouldn't happen to have any white wine in that fridge, would you?" Maren asks, prodding Scarlett's side and wiggling her eyebrows. Clearly, their small moving-related fight is over.

"Mmm, no, but I can have Caleb stop and pick some up on his way over."

Maren and I exchange a look.

"Caleb's coming over?" I arch a suggestive brow.

Scarlett shrugs innocently, holding her phone tightly to her chest. "He's a good friend of mine, actually. We've known each other since college."

Interesting. I'd assumed Scarlet first made friends with the girls in the group. I didn't realize Caleb was one of her oldest friends.

Maren gives her an appraising look, perching on the edge of the couch. "You guys have been hanging out a lot," she says delicately. "Anything going on there?"

"With Caleb?" Scarlett's eyebrows jump. "God, no. Can you imagine?"

A mischievous grin spreads across Maren's face. Apparently, she *can* imagine. But not knowing Caleb's personality well, I have no idea what exactly she's imagining.

In the few interactions we've had, he seems funny and chill. But now I'm wondering if he has a revolving bedroom door of a past like Connor apparently did.

"I invited a few people over to see the new place," Scarlett says, waving one hand.

My stomach leaps. To Scarlett, "a few people" probably means the majority of her friend group. The majority of her friend group means the men of Frisky Business, and the men of Frisky Business means Connor, who I haven't seen or spoken to since he kissed me on his birthday.

Yeah, let's just say that's one detail I've left out of this girls' evening so far. Not that I think Maren and Scarlett would disapprove. Quite the opposite.

I just don't think I'm ready to spill the tea with them about Connor yet. Especially not when I still haven't found a solution to the whole "I'm leaving you and your baby girl in a few months" situation. Nope, I've made my bed. Now I've just got to lie in it. Even if that means lying in it alone.

"Okay, so . . . pizza toppings?" I say with a smile.

"Get the roasted garlic, four cheese and truffle oil, and two of the Turkish lamb pizzas," Scarlett says. "I'll pay you back."

"Lamb pizza?" I ask.

Scarlett lobs a serious look my way. "Believe me, it's the best thing you will ever put in your mouth."

"True story," Maren says with a nod.

I place the order on my phone and select delivery, because who in the heck wants to go out right now?

"Pizza has been ordered," I say.

"Thanks, girl," Scarlett says a second before her

phone buzzes, and she lets out an excited squeal.

"Hellooo?" she answers, her voice an excited singsong. Her face falls slightly. "Oh. Sure, I'll let you up."

Maren and I give her the same curious look. "It's Connor," Scarlett mouths with a halfhearted shrug.

I can feel Maren watching my face for a reaction, but I'm too busy wondering if Scarlett's excited reaction was because she thought it would be Caleb.

Scarlett disappears down the hallway, her footsteps fading before the distant sound of a door slamming alerts us that she found him successfully. Their footsteps approach quickly, and my heartbeat races to catch up with them. When Scarlett bursts through the door, she has her hostess face on, all bright smiles and warm sashays.

"Our first guest has arrived," she sings again, waving for Connor to enter.

Speak of the devil, and apparently he will appear with a bottle of rosé. How thoughtful.

Connor steps through the doorway looking as gorgeous as ever, his dark hair pushed back off his forehead, a gray T-shirt revealing the subtle outline of his muscles. His green eyes find mine within seconds, and a shock wave of heat passes through my core.

Down, girl.

Yes, he's attractive and fit, and did I mention before how long it's been since I've gotten any? But none of these thoughts are the least bit helpful right now. I'm only here for a short time, and I'm certainly not going to get wrapped up in *anyone* before I leave the country. And least of all my new boss.

"Wow, nice place, Scar," he says, surveying the kitchen briefly before his gaze lands on Maren, and then me. "Hey, Maren. Hi, Jessa."

I smile weakly at him and wave.

Oh my God. Did I just wave at him? Sweet Jesus, kill me now.

I'm never normally this awk-weird, but ever since we woke up tangled together in that hotel bed, I'm majorly off my game. And now add making out to the mix, I'm acting like a thirteen-year-old crushing on the most popular boy in school.

Yep. Kill me now.

Scarlett whisks Connor away to give him the grand tour of her new place, which will probably take all of two minutes. While they're gone, I turn to Maren, who's still eyeing me with playful suspicion.

"I'm thinking it's definitely time for a drink," I say quickly. "Are you with me?"

She nods and takes my hand, leading me into the kitchen. "So, you wanna talk about it?"

Maren's been the sweet one from the beginning, someone I know I can talk to about these things. She knows better than anyone what it's like to have complicated feelings for someone. Maybe it would be a good idea for me to open up to her. To talk to someone about the craziness swirling around in my head. Girl talk would do me a world of good.

"Well, I guess it's just—"

But before I can finish, the front door to the apartment bangs open, followed by a chorus of hoots and hollers. My eyes grow wide and I stare at Maren, shock and worry all over my face, but she just smiles and rolls her eyes.

"The boys must be here. They can get a little . . . rowdy when they're all together. It'll pass after the first, like, twenty minutes, though," she says, clearly noticing that the worry on my face didn't fade away. It sounds like a freaking rugby game is being played in Scarlett's front hallway.

Drinks in hand, we walk back out into the living room to find that the rest of the "get-together" has arrived. And now that everyone is all in one place, we might as well call this what it is—a housewarming party. Scarlett's having a party, a small impromptu one, sure, but a party nonetheless. Meanwhile, it's taking all my self-control not to melt in Connor's presence, even with the rest of the crew here.

Maren is quick to close the distance between herself and Hayes, and he lifts her into his arms and plants a sweet kiss on her mouth.

One day, I hope to be so in love that I can make out in front of a room full of people without caring that everyone else can see. It would be sweet if it didn't happen every time they see each other. I can only imagine what their reunions are like when it's just the two of them. That's love for you, I guess.

Connor makes his way across the room to me, and my pulse quickens with every step closer he takes. "Hey," he says when he reaches my side.

His wrist almost brushes mine, we're standing so close. I have to keep myself from trembling.

"Hey," I say back.

He looks at me apologetically. "I didn't really say hi to you before."

"That's okay," I say with a smile and a shrug. "It's good to see you. How's Marley?"

I've never sounded so stiff, so polite around him before. But I'm not exactly sure where we stand after the last time we saw each other. Besides, we're with his friends now, and they're quickly becoming my friends too. So, whatever's happening between Connor and me can take a back seat to hanging out with the crew.

"With her mom," he says. "Marley misses you, I think."

I freeze. Or maybe whatever's happening between Connor and me will be the only thing I think about all night.

Is he actually talking about his baby, who barely recognizes human faces yet? Or is this some kind of code for the fact that *he* misses me? But that can't be right, can it?

Does Connor miss me? Is he trying to tell me something?

Feeling his gaze on me, I take a sip of my wine, grateful for the cool bite of the liquid going down my throat.

Penelope appears from the kitchen, a sullen-looking Wolfie in tow. "Connor," she says quickly, rushing toward us. "How's my niece? Please tell me you have pictures."

Connor nods. "What kind of dad would I be if I didn't? Hey, Wolf, did you grab one of the IPAs from the fridge?"

Wolfie grunts and jerks his chin. Apparently, that means yes, because Connor and Penelope turn back to Connor's phone, leaving me to smile awkwardly at Wolfie. He's so big . . . and so quiet, sort of like a big teddy bear. I'm really not sure what to make of him.

"So," I say, clasping my hands in front of my waist. "How's life?"

Wolfie grimaces slightly.

I've been told he hates small talk more than the rest of the guys, but I can't help it. What am I supposed to do, stand here in awkward silence and wait for Connor and Penelope to be done gushing about the baby? I'm not about to interrupt their sibling time. I'm trying to make a good impression here, after all.

"It's good," Wolfie says and takes a long pull from his beer bottle.

Thankfully, Connor and Penelope resurface from the phone quickly, and the three of us start chatting easily.

Penelope and Wolfie are quite the odd couple, that's for sure, but it's hard not to be taken with Penelope's kindness. She's just one of the nicest people I've ever met. It's easy to see how she and Connor are related, especially with the two of them standing right next to each other. They have the same bone structure, the same easy smiles. And Penelope's sharp, like her brother. She may be young, but that doesn't mean she's one to underestimate.

"Please tell me my brother's not taking advantage of you," she says with a playful arch to her brow.

"I . . . what?" I look between Penelope and Connor. Did he say something to her? Are they really that close of siblings? But Connor looks as panic stricken as I feel.

"I'm kidding." She punches Connor in the arm, and my face relaxes into a smile.

I chuckle without really even meaning to, and he and I share a passing glance that communicates everything we were both thinking in an instant—*thank fucking God.*

"No, he's a good boss, and a good dad." I glance at him again and a small smile curls my lips. "Even if he can be a little overly stressed sometimes. Did he tell you about last week when he thought Marley had scarlet fever?"

"Oh, Con, no," Penelope says, giving her brother a sympathetic look.

"It's still a thing, you know," Connor says, protesting weakly.

Penelope and I give him reassuring looks.

"Marley's lucky to have you," I say, and without thinking about it, I place my hand on his arm. After a second, I pull away, but my hand feels electric just from touching him.

Connor holds my gaze a second longer than necessary, and when I look away, I catch Penelope studying us. She gives me a curious smile, and I pull my lips into the blandest, most innocent smile I can manage. The last thing I need right now is Connor's sister getting any ideas about what's happening between us.

What is happening between us?

Nothing, I quickly decide. It was one hot kiss. And some lingering chemistry, but how *wouldn't* there be? Connor's young, fit, and attractive. That's all. It's nothing I can't handle.

Wolfie loops an arm around Penelope's waist. "Give us the grand tour, Scar."

Scarlett grins and leads the way, pointing out features of her new place—like the cozy dining nook, and the built-in shelves in the hallway—until we end up in the guest bedroom. "Look, plenty of room for you idiots to stay over and crash if someone has too much to drink."

"I call dibs on the guest room," Caleb says, flopping his big body onto the queen mattress.

Wolfie raises one eyebrow. "Well, this room is claimed."

"What about me?" Connor grumbles. "Do you have a pullout for me?"

"We all know you don't pull out," Caleb says with a playful look, and everyone dissolves into laughter.

"Ha-ha, fuckers," Connor mutters, frowning, and I suppress a laugh.

As the tour winds down, we end up back in Scarlett's living room. Hayes and Maren squeeze onto the same armchair, Penelope and Wolfie sit closely on the couch with Scarlett nearby, and Caleb takes a seat near Scarlett's feet, leaving Connor and me to fight it out for the last armchair.

"Oh, do you want to sit here?" I gesture to the chair. I can feel Penelope and Maren watching us, even as the rest of the group laughs and continues talking loudly over us.

Connor nods for me to sit. "No, go for it."

"No, really, you should take it," I say, insisting.

"Oh, for fuck's sake." Scarlett throws her hands in the air. "One of you grab one of the stools from the kitchen and sit down already."

A blush burns my cheeks.

Connor runs a hand over the back of his neck and walks to the kitchen in a few short strides. He returns with one of Scarlett's tall silver bar stools with sleek black seats. He sets it down next to the big chair and takes a seat, and I curl up in the plush armchair.

Wolfie watches our entire interaction with interest.

Is it just me, or is Wolfie weirdly perceptive sometimes?

The doorbell rings and the pizza arrives. Scarlett sets the boxes on the table between us, and we descend on the food like hungry vultures. Clearly, everyone worked hard today, whether that work included selling vibrators and dildos to very horny people, or moving Scarlett's life two neighborhoods over.

The conversation shifts from teasing Connor to Maren's work to whether or not it's acceptable to dip pizza in ranch dressing. Another two hours pass, eating and drinking and talking with my new friends, and before I even know it, it's almost midnight.

Just a few weeks ago, I moved to a temporary new place, expecting to detach from my life in Chicago and start a new one thousands of miles away. But lately, it's getting harder and harder to remember why I decided to go to Central America in the first place.

I like my life here, even if it's not a normal nine-to-five job. I have friends and a place to live, and . . . well, there's Connor. I feel like I fit here, more than I realized. Maybe more than I have any place before.

And I don't know if I'm ready to give that all up just yet.

Nine

CONNOR

Turns out, all it takes for me to act on a very, very bad idea is a little peer pressure.

Well, more like nonstop pressure from my peers—in person during work, over text after work, and all throughout the weekend. The onslaught can be summarized in one simple question: *When are you gonna ask Jessa out?*

I haven't been able to stop thinking about our kiss. If this were one of the movies Penelope likes to watch, that one kiss would have had life-changing effects on the protagonists.

But this isn't a movie.

This is real life, and to be honest, it shocked me how perfect Jessa's mouth felt on mine and the soft noises she made when I deepened our kiss. I can't explain the rush of emotions that left me breathless and wanting more. The truth is, I'm lonely, and for a lot more than just sex.

And as crazy as it sounds, I think my friends are right. The only way I'm going to survive this overwhelming attraction to the nanny is to finally take her out on a date. Maybe it's just the taboo aspect of it all that has me sex-crazy for her. Maybe we'll have zero chemistry, and we can file this one away under awkward mistakes and move the fuck on with our lives.

Or maybe this is my best shot at something real.

"Hellooo, Earth to Connor . . ."

Jessa's musical voice snaps me back to the present, where we're sorting and labeling frozen baggies of Beth's breast milk on the kitchen counter. She gave me a whole cooler's worth when I dropped off Marley last night for the weekend. Not exactly the most romantic of circumstances to ask someone out on a first date, but I'll take what I can get.

"Sorry, what were you saying?"

"Nothing," Jessa says with a laugh. "You were in the middle of telling a story about Hayes and Wolfie and how they grew up together?"

My heart swells a little at the familiarity with which she talks about my best friends. She was amazing with everyone the other night, totally natural and in sync with their joke slinging and name calling. Honestly, that may have been what cinched the deal for me on this whole date idea.

"Shit." I chuckle, setting another bag into the freezer. "My bad. My mind's wandering."

"You need a break," Jessa says solemnly.

"I was thinking the same thing. We both need a break," I say, proud of myself for this smooth-as-hell transition. "Actually, I was thinking about going on a date."

"Oh, okay. Yep, you should." Her gaze flits to mine for a second before locking back onto the measuring cups. "I'm good to watch Marley whenever."

Wait. What? Jessa thinks I meant a date with someone else.

Fuck. That's my bad for being vague.

"No, I mean . . ." I reach for her hand, instantly regretting the electricity-inducing contact and craving it in equal measure. "You and me. Would you like to go on a date . . . with me?"

Jessa is shocked speechless. With each second

that passes as I wait for her response, I'm closer to throwing myself through the nearest window.

Is this wildly inappropriate? Have I just lost my nanny?

Finally, she blinks, and her lips purse into a secretive little smile. She tugs at my hand playfully. "You mean us? Like going on a date-date?"

"Yeah. A date-date. If you're up for it."

"Well, duh," she blurts.

I can't help the grin that breaks out across my face. I'm so fucking relieved, and she's *so* fucking cute.

She tucks an unruly strand of hair behind her ear before asking, "When?"

"You free tonight?"

"Yeah." Jessa chuckles, all sparkling eyes and blushing cheeks. "What did you have in mind?"

Shit. I hadn't thought that far.

"I'm thinking dinner. Drinks. My treat. How does that sound to you?"

"Good." She sighs happily, and damn, do I love that sound.

"Good."

I echo the sentiment, enjoying the way the sunlight peeks through the blinds and lights up the freckles across her nose. Never mind the fact that we're shamelessly flirting before eight in the morning.

Glancing at the clock, I wince. "You think you can handle the rest of this? I should head to work."

"Sure. Storing your ex's breast milk is a lot easier than I thought it'd be." The words come out so fast that Jessa only realizes how strange they are a moment too late. She scrunches her eyes closed and recovers with a sheepish smile. "Yes, I mean."

"Great." I chuckle, squeezing her hand. "I'll see you later."

The whole drive downtown, I grin like a little kid on Christmas morning. By the time I reach the shop, my face is actually sore from all the smiling. I guess it's been a while since I used these muscles for a stretch. Jessa brings that out in me.

Throughout the workday, that stocking-stuffer giddiness dissolves into a nagging concern that I jumped into this too quickly.

Dinner and drinks are fine, sure, but where should I take her? What kind of place would Jessa enjoy?

I'm struggling to come up with a plan for tonight without falling back on old date ideas. Hayes is off today, so I make the mistake of asking Wolfie and Caleb for their input on how to make this night special.

"Erotic body painting," Caleb says, his expression a little too casual for comfort. It doesn't help that he's currently juggling Ben Wa balls, and has been doing so for the past hour.

I roll my eyes. "Okay . . . next."

"You could just stay in. Cook dinner. Watch a movie," Wolfie grumbles, ever the homebody.

"Jessa and I spend all of our time at home. I want to do something she's going to remember." Preferably with a happy little smile on her lips when she thinks of it. Of me.

But all I get is a shrug in response.

I groan, leaning against the stockroom door. "Guys, you know I'm out of practice. I need serious ideas."

I wish Hayes weren't conveniently absent, or else I'd hound him instead. Or have him ask Rosie, his grandmother. Or even Maren. They're all romantics, so they'd have this figured out in no time at all.

"Oh shit. I've got it," Caleb says, dropping all of the balls with a clatter to snap his fingers like some corny cartoon character. He digs into his back pocket and pulls out two small postcards. "Fuck yeah, this is the best idea *ever*. You're welcome."

I take the postcards, hoping against all hope that Caleb will for once prove to be useful. "'Spice Up Your Sex Life,'" I read with a frown. "'A workshop for curious couples.' Dude, *no*."

"Why? It's the first class of our workshop series. It's gonna be dope."

"Because this is a *first date*, you lunatic."

"Then what about the other one?"

Lifting the second card, I raise an eyebrow at the words I'm reading. BLOW-JOB BASICS. The glare I shoot Caleb could turn him to stone. "Do you wanna die?"

He lifts his hands in surrender. "You asked me. If you don't want advice from the modern-day Casanova, don't ask him."

I roll my eyes. Fucking hopeless.

I fold the cards in half and stuff them into my pocket. The last thing I need is to add any more fuel to the burning sexual desire I feel for Jessa. Out of sight, out of mind.

Before I leave the shop, I shoot Jessa a text asking her to meet me at the house. I text back and forth with her for a bit about dress code and logistics without giving away too much of the plan. When I get home, she's already sitting on my front porch, wearing a dark purple dress and a simple pair of black flats.

"Hey," she calls over the hum of cicadas with a smile and a short wave.

"Hey," I say, walking up the steps. "You look incredible."

My low voice probably gives away exactly how attracted to her I am. Don't get me wrong, she even looks incredible in yoga pants and a T-shirt with spit-up down the front. But this outfit has my heart fluttering like a caged butterfly.

Jessa cocks her head, her hair tumbling over one shoulder like a chocolate fountain. "Thank you."

When I get closer to let her inside, I note the dark lipstick accentuating her already plush lips. She smiles when she catches me staring. The girl is hot as hell, and I'm pretty sure she knows it.

I grin back, swinging the door open and bowing my head like some sort of Victorian dandy making way for a queen. The gesture earns me a lilting laugh that echoes down the hallway of my home. Tonight is going to be fun.

"This is what I'm thinking. We head back down Lakeshore Drive toward the shop, and have dinner and drinks at this upscale little patio bistro down the block. Then when we're done, we can take a walk down to the lakefront and watch the sunset. What do you think?"

"Sure, sounds like fun to me." She grins, leaning over one of the dining room chairs, her cleavage peeking out of the top of her dress. *Hot damn.* "You've got the whole night planned out, don't you? For once, you don't need my help," she teases.

"Untrue. How about this . . . you're in charge of what we order," I say, splaying my hands on the table like we're making a very serious business deal.

Jessa purses her lips and pretends to ponder this for a moment. "Works for me," she says with a shrug, that mischievous smile sparkling through her eyes.

With a smile, I empty the contents of my pockets out on the table. "Can you give me five minutes so I can change, and then we can—"

"What's that?" She points to the postcards I just tossed on the table between us.

Shit.

"Oh, ah, yeah . . . Frisky Business has this new initiative where we're offering classes to the public. Sex education, more or less. I'm not really involved; it's Caleb's project."

"Wow," Jessa murmurs, picking up the postcards and scanning them.

I'm still scrambling for something else to say when she lifts one card, flipping it toward me.

"This one is tonight. 'Spice Up Your Sex Life' at eight o'clock."

"Yeah," I say with a grunt. *Goddammit, Caleb.*

"Cool. Looks interesting." When she lifts her gaze to find me standing there like a dead-eyed mannequin, she squints in confusion. "Did you still want to change?"

"Shit. Yeah, just give me a minute," I say like an idiot.

I shuffle back toward my room, a little in shock. I didn't peg Jessa as someone who'd think a class called "Spice Up Your Sex Life" is a cool or interesting thing. Frankly, I didn't find it cool or interesting until I heard the words fall out of her delicious mouth. Now I can't stop thinking about it.

In my room, I quickly whip off my T-shirt and change into a short-sleeve button-up and a pair of dark-wash jeans. Catching a glance of myself in the mirror, I cringe at my haircut. It's grown out substantially, the dark strands starting to curl across my forehead and around my ears. Not a lot of time to keep everything looking sharp when you're a single dad.

I rub some product between my palms and style my hair back into some semblance of order. One spritz of cologne later, and I'm ready to go.

Back in the dining room, Jessa looks up from her phone, her cheeks turning pink when she sees me. "You look nice," she murmurs with a tilt of her head.

I laugh and thank her before I help her to her feet. Grabbing my keys from the bowl on our way out the door, I take her hand and don't let go.

Despite it being a Friday night, the patio isn't overpacked, large enough to comfortably seat a decent-sized crowd. We're served quickly, and before long, two mounds of butternut squash casserole sit on plates before us, steaming with the promise of a damn good meal. It's difficult to remember to eat my own food, watching Jessa wrap her lips around each delicious bite.

When she finishes, she lets out a little moan and happily squirms in her seat. "I've gotta learn how to make this."

The waiter comes by, topping off our glasses of merlot with a smile.

When he's left the table with our empty plates and my credit card, she leans in and whispers, "Dear God, how much wine have we had already? I can't keep track when he's coming around every two minutes to make sure my glass is always full."

I lean in, mirroring her movements. "Oh, I have no idea. I thought it was your job to monitor our drinking tonight," I whisper back with mock concern, and she swats me playfully on the arm.

"You're right. I only had one job," she fake laments, the low-hanging string lights reflecting the humorous sparkle in her eyes.

I love to see Jessa carefree like this. I lean back in my seat, the wine buzz making me more sentimental than usual.

"You've got a funny look on your face," she says softly, gazing at me from over the rim of her glass. "What are you thinking about?"

Falling in love with you. The thought is so immediate and unexpected that I have to bite my lower lip to keep the words from slipping off my tongue. That's the merlot talking.

"I'm thinking about . . ." I say the words slowly, stalling for a few more seconds as she waits patiently with a knowing smile, giving me all the time in the world to respond to the simplest of questions. "How glad I am that you and I are here tonight. Together."

There. Honest, without showing all my cards just yet.

"I'm glad too," she says warmly, tilting her head to the side so her curls bounce in an adorable way. "Thanks for asking me out."

I tilt my head to match hers. "Thanks for saying yes."

The waiter returns with my card and I settle the bill, aware of Jessa's eyes on me the whole time. We talk for another hour until the final drops in our wineglasses have disappeared.

When we stand, Jessa steps closer to me. I usually don't like when people invade my personal space, but when it's Jessa doing it . . . hell, she could step on my toes any day of the week.

She looks up at me through her long dark eyelashes. "What's next?"

"How does the lakefront sound?"

"Honestly?" Jessa frowns, crossing her arms over her chest. "Kind of chilly."

I could kick myself for not bringing a jacket on the off chance she'd need one. Goes to show you how out of practice I am at this stuff.

"True. Want to head back then?" I reach for my phone in my back pocket to call a car.

"I'm not ready to go home yet," she murmurs, her gaze wandering to the glowing city lights around us.

I'm not either.

"What about checking out that class then?" I hear myself asking the question, but I'm as surprised as she is when the words leave my mouth.

What the hell, Connor? How much wine have I had?

Jessa's already wine-tinted cheeks deepen with color, her blue eyes focused on my lower lip. Just when I think she might lean in, she bursts into laughter.

"You know what? Yes. Let's go. Why not, right?" The look on her face is absolutely joyous and completely infectious.

I'm grinning back at her when I scoop her hand into mine and lead us down the road back toward Frisky Business. The walk is short and pleasant, the night breeze cool enough that Jessa tucks herself against my arm.

All is perfect until we step into the shop and walk smack dab into a garish display of dildos under a sign that reads:

COMPLIMENTARY. THANKS FOR JOINING US!

Whose fucking idea . . .

Caleb. It's got to be. Fucking Caleb.

The look of pure shock on Jessa's face has me swimming in a pool of regret. I'm such a fucking jackass. Way to ruin an otherwise perfect night. I'm about to spew some lame apology when the instructor emerges from the back and waves us inside.

"Y'all here for the sex-ed class? Come on in, folks. Welcome."

Still cursing silently, I follow Jessa to the back

of the store where a gathering of couples are mingling around the coffee machine situated just outside the meeting room. Jessa turns back to me, the expression on her face equal parts excitement and trepidation.

"No turning back now, huh?" she whispers, a familiar sparkle returning to her eyes.

I'd have to agree. I think we're well past the point of no return now.

Ten

JESSA

This has officially become the most unique date I've ever been on.

We're sitting in the back room at Frisky Business with six other couples. By "we," I mean I'm sitting next to Connor, who's looking so hot it's unfair. His knee is so close to mine that I can almost feel the heat of his skin through the denim of his jeans. Between the closeness of his body and the fact that we're literally sitting in the back of a sex-toy shop that he owns, it's getting really, really hard to focus.

I'll admit, when Connor first asked me out, I was hesitant. Scratch that. I didn't even realize what he was asking. He's my boss, after all, and our dating would be totally inappropriate. Plus, with every day that passes, I get closer to leaving, and that doesn't feel fair to Connor or to baby Marley.

But then Connor looked at me, and I looked back at him, and the look in those dreamy green eyes was enough to make my heart ooze out of my chest.

I know what it's like to feel rejection. Real rejection. The kind that pierces through you, pokes holes in your chest, makes you feel like you're empty and hollow inside. And I knew I couldn't do that to him. Not to Connor. Not to a man who's so sweet, so sincere, he makes me wonder why I ever wanted to leave this city.

Because I've been with men who were the opposite of him. Men who were cruel and heartless and cold. Men who rejected me, even when they were with me. Men who looked for every opportunity to tear me down, to make me feel small and insignificant and unworthy of their precious attention. I've wasted years chasing after those kinds of men, waiting for them to change, waiting for them to love me the way I wanted them to.

But of course they never did. No amount of love I could give them could ever be enough. They were who they were, and I had to accept that. Or, in my case, have them push me away so many times I felt like I might break into a million tiny insignificant pieces until I decided to stop crawling back to them anymore.

Then finally, one day I started to put myself back together again. I took some time for myself, a year or two, to really figure out who I was and what I wanted. That's how I'd decided on the trip to Central America.

It wasn't just about getting away—it was about helping people, doing something that really mattered. Which is why it feels so terrible that any part of me is now thinking about staying in Chicago after all. Even if it is for Connor. Going on the trip is supposed to be for me. It's supposed to be a part of my healing.

"Friends, lovers, people of all varieties, welcome to Spice Up Your Sex Life." A twenty-something woman with lavender hair, a septum ring, and an artful half sleeve on her left arm stands at the front of the room with her hands clasped over her heart, and a warm, welcoming smile on her face. "I'm Neda, and I'll be your guide this evening."

Neda starts walking around the room, weaving through the rows of couples as she continues.

"Everyone's spice levels are going to be different. Anything outside of missionary might be spicy for some. Others might have a closet full of whips and chains. We're all approaching things from different angles, and wherever you're coming from, that's okay. I still think everyone will get something out of this class."

Her gaze lands directly on me when she says the word "everyone." Or at least, it feels like her gaze is on me.

Is it hot in here? Am I the only one sweating?

I turn to sneak a peek at Connor's face, only to find him peering down at me to check mine. I quirk a brow up at him. He holds up his hands and murmurs, "There are no whips or chains in my closet. I promise."

I bite my lip to stifle a nervous giggle. *All right, then. It's going to be that kind of evening.*

"Before we get started, let's get to know each other," Neda says, casting a broad smile around the room. "How long has everyone been with their partner?"

The man in the couple next to us speaks first. "Eight years."

Oh shit.

"Fourteen," someone says from behind us.

"Two of the best years of my life," a woman

says at the front of the room, placing her hand on her partner's shoulder.

The instructor reaches our row and stares at Connor and me expectantly. We exchange a look, and he shrugs.

"This is our first date," he says somewhat shyly.

A few of the couples around us cheer, and Neda gives us an impressed smile.

"Adventure. Good. That bodes well for your future," she says mysteriously before whisking herself away to the front of the room.

She plants herself in front of the couple who's been together for two years, and they stare up at her admiringly.

"So," Neda says briskly, "tonight we'll be focusing primarily on the concept of accelerators and brakes. Accelerators are things that heat you up. Brakes, on the other hand, are things that make you . . . not in the mood."

My stomach drops. I'm not sure what I was expecting from a class called "Spice Up Your Sex Life" that takes place in the back of a sex-toy shop, but it's only hitting me right now just how intimate these topics will be. Dangerously close to being too intimate to discuss with someone I've only known for a few weeks and shared a single kiss with.

But strangely, as Neda keeps talking, explaining examples of accelerators, nothing about this feels awkward. I can't imagine being here with anyone except Connor. Instead of discomfort or strained silence between the two of us, there's this buzzy excitement, like we can't wait to get started.

Although, let's be honest, the alcohol might have had something to do with that.

The instructor continues to wander around the room, this time handing out a worksheet to each of the couples. She places one of the papers on the table in front of us, and Connor and I exchange a look.

"Use this worksheet to start a discussion between you and your partner. It's important to communicate about your accelerators and your brakes. Otherwise, you might not realize when you're pressing both pedals at the same time."

She arches a brow at us and then continues around the room, and a low hum of muted voices fills the air as the couples begin discussing.

Connor picks up the sheet of paper, scanning the questions before looking back at me. There's a playful glint in his eyes, coupled with something curious, something darker. My stomach ties itself into a thousand tiny knots, and I lick my lips and nod for him to read.

His eyebrows shoot up, and then he smiles. It's a rare smile, the kind that makes me want to melt into a puddle of warm mush. Then he clears his throat and asks, "What's an accelerator for you? The examples are watching porn together, lighting candles, wearing lingerie . . . role-playing games?"

My mouth falls open. *This*. This is an accelerator for me. Hearing Connor's deep voice rumble over each word.

I quickly pull myself together. Tossing my hair over my shoulder, I look up at the ceiling and bite my lip, trying to look like I'm thinking. "Wearing lingerie," I say finally. "And lighting candles. Porn is kind of *take it or leave it* for me."

Connor nods slowly, and I can practically see him struggling not to ogle every inch of my body. "Lingerie is good."

I laugh softly and take the paper from his hands. Clearly, we're not going to get any further with that line of questioning. "What about your brakes? Knowing there's a mess in the house, feeling like there's pressure to perform? According to this, a car won't go if you're pressing the accelerator and the brake is still on."

"Brakes?" He considers the question for a moment, then says, "If anything's wrong with Marley. Or if I'm worried there's anything wrong with Marley."

I nod. "That makes sense."

"You?"

"I guess I would say a dirty bedroom."

Connor snorts. "I'm sorry, what?"

"Have you seen the inside of a twenty-something male's bedroom lately? It's tragic. And a major turnoff."

He shakes his head, laughing harder this time. "I apologize on behalf of my entire gender."

I turn back to the paper, genuinely curious for his answer to this next question. "What about the goals of sex?" I ask, tilting my head to the side.

"Well, I think that one's pretty obvious. Orgasms, clearly," he says with a chuckle, and I stare back at him. When I don't immediately agree, he asks, "Why? What do you think?"

"Don't get me wrong, orgasms are great and definitely important. But I also think that sex can be about feeling close to someone in a really authentic way."

I hadn't even fully thought it through before I said it, but once the words come out, I know I mean them. I love an endorphin rush as much as the next girl, but that closeness? That's something else altogether.

Connor makes a noise of agreement and nods, a soft smile spreading across his face. "I like that."

Sometimes I wish he wouldn't say such sweet and dangerous things. If he didn't, it would be a whole lot easier to pretend that I'm not feeling half the things I'm feeling. Pretending is something I've gotten pretty good at these days.

"Okay, my turn," he says, taking the paper back and glancing down at it. "This next round is a series of questions that you answer *yes*, *no*, or *maybe*. To make it as fair as possible, let's say our answers at the same time, okay?"

I give him a disbelieving look. "How do I know I can trust you?"

Connor's expression is more sincere than I was expecting. "You're just going to have to."

All right then, I guess I will.

"The first item on the list is bondage. So we'll say our answer on the count of three. One, two, three . . ."

"No," we say in perfect unison.

We blink at each other, and he smiles.

"Told you there were no whips or chains in my closet."

I roll my eyes. "What's next on the list?"

"Sixty-nining," he says, his eyes growing dark. "One, two, three . . ."

"Yes," we both say.

A blush creeps over my cheeks. That's a mental image I'll be thinking of for quite some time.

But Connor carries on, clearly determined to find out our compatibility according to this list. "Trying new positions. One, two, three."

"Yes," we both say.

"Bringing toys into the bedroom. Is this even a question for me?" he asks with a devilish smile.

"Oh, so you're saying you get high on your own supply?" I grin, leaning in toward him.

"That," he says, mirroring my position, so that our faces are only inches apart, "is exactly what I'm saying."

My breath catches in my chest, my gaze falling to his mouth. His lips are full and just begging for me to kiss them. But before I can make good on that thought, he pulls away, turning back to the paper.

"Anal?" he asks.

"What?" I almost sputter. *Breathe, Jessa.*

He cocks his head to the side. "It's the next item on the list. Anal. One, two, three."

The gears in my head are barely working, so I stumble out a "maybe," and I'm surprised to hear Connor say the same. Surprise is on his face too. I guess there's a lot we agree on.

"Opening up the relationship," he says flatly. "One, two, three."

"No." Both of our voices are decisive and firm.

He nods and turns the sheet over. "I guess that's it. We did it."

"That wasn't so bad. I was expecting it to be much more scandalous."

He smiles, raising one brow. "Do you want me to ask you some scandalous questions to make up for it?"

I give him a light shove, my skin electric where it meets his. He pretends to fall over, but then sits back up and places his hand on my knee, and now I really feel like my skin's on fire.

The instructor gives us some final words of encouragement, telling us to take everything we learned back to the bedroom tonight, and sends us off into the summer evening.

Connor takes my hand on the walk back to our neighborhood. I try to pretend it's a small, sweet gesture, one that doesn't really have to mean anything. He's just trying to make sure that I'm safe. That I don't blow away in the summer breeze.

But him holding my hand has nothing to do with the heat that's been pulsing between us all night, or the way my voice catches in my throat for a moment every time he looks me in the eye. When he takes my hand, it feels like the most natural thing in the world, and I don't know if I'll ever be able to let go.

"So, that was interesting," he says. His palm is warm against mine, and his fingers settle over my knuckles.

"It was," I say with a slight tilt of my head. "Very . . . enlightening."

The only sounds around us are the rumble of cars, the hum of cicadas, and our footsteps in sync on the sidewalk. My heart thuds against my chest, and I almost wonder if Connor can feel my pulse in my wrist. I'd try to relax, but I don't know if that's possible.

Thankfully, it's a short drive home, and it's not long before we're standing on the sidewalk in front of mine. I glance up at the doorway and back at Connor, who's giving me a shy smile.

"Sorry if tonight was weird. I haven't been on a date in forever," he says, looking down at his feet.

His tone is sincere, apologetic even, and my heart cracks a little at the thought of him believing any of that.

"It wasn't weird," I say, taking a step toward him and searching his gaze. "I had a nice time, Connor. Really, I did."

He looks up, and suddenly, I'm aware of just how close I've made us. Close enough that I can feel his breath on my cheeks and see the flecks of gold mixed with the green of his eyes.

His gaze meets mine before flitting down to my mouth, and in one motion, Connor takes his hand to the back of my neck and pulls me in closer to him. Our lips touch, and at first it's soft and search- ing like a question. He moves slowly, taking his time.

Every lingering doubt I've had about what's happening between us slips away, and his kiss sends a shock from my lips straight through to my core. A burning, hungry need lights up inside me, and I answer by touching my fingertips to the stubble on his jaw and kissing him back, deeper than before.

I can't tell you how long we stand there in the driveway, wrapped in each other's arms, but when we finally part, the world feels different. It's like the temperature dropped a few degrees and the air grew damp and heady. Connor's eyes twinkle as he tucks a stray curl into place behind my ear, and my body screams for him to touch me again.

His voice is low and husky when he asks, "Do you want to come inside?"

Eleven

CONNOR

The front door has barely latched closed behind us before I have Jessa pressed up against the wall, my knee wedged between her parted thighs.

Our mouths are locked in a kiss unlike any I've ever experienced—new and exciting, and yet somehow so familiar, like we've kissed a thousand times before. But the truth is, save for my drunken advances, this is the first time we've ever let ourselves be this close. This honest. This real.

And let me tell you, after torturous weeks of imagining this very scenario? Reality most certainly takes the cake. Because this is fucking phenomenal. Her mouth. Her tongue. Her taste. Her breath. Everything Jessa.

She rakes her fingers through my hair, the

damn-near music of her needy little moans echoing down the front hall. I've never been more excited to have the house all to myself . . . to not be concerned about waking Marley up. The thought of Jessa screaming my name later tonight in the throes of passion sparks a fire deep in my groin. We can be as loud as we want to be.

I pull back, catching my breath. Her eyes flutter open to meet mine as I smooth a few stray hairs from her freckled face.

"Jessa?" Her name feels so good on my tongue.

"Yeah?" She's breathless and sounds just as turned on as I feel.

"Is this okay?" I caress her cheek.

She responds by nipping my thumb, her eyes sparkling with mischief. And when her tongue sneaks out from between her pink lips to swipe against my fingertip, my mouth goes bone dry. She hasn't even touched my dick yet, and I'm already as hard as a goddamn telephone pole. Safe to say my libido is back, full throttle, ready to be unleashed on the gorgeous nanny.

"Does that answer your question?" Jessa whispers seductively, leaning into me to nuzzle the tip of her nose against my cheek. Meanwhile, her hands explore the muscles of my shoulders and chest, leaving a trail of goose bumps in their wake.

"Point taken," I murmur against her ear, my lips brushing along the curve of it before I nibble on her earlobe.

She shudders beneath me, her hips moving into mine until she's grinding herself against my leg like a cat in heat. Within seconds, her fingers are pulling at the buttons of my shirt.

You don't have to tell me twice.

I dip down to scoop Jessa's thighs up, my fingers pressing into the bare skin of her soft-as-sin legs. Her dress scrunches up around her waist and her feet dangle in the air behind me as I lift her, one shoe falling off her foot and hitting the floor with a thud as she wraps her long limbs around my hips.

I push her against the wall more confidently now, groaning when I feel the hot center of her core against my abdomen. While Jessa pulls my shirt loose from my pants, popping button after button, I make it my life's mission to taste every square inch of her neck. When I find a particularly sensitive spot, just over the fluttering of her pulse, Jessa arches her back and murmurs in approval.

"Oh wow, that's good," she whispers, and the words make my desire for her swell even more than I thought possible.

Fuck. My dick strains against the zipper of my jeans, desperate for her. *Slow down, Connor.*

"Should I take us into my bedroom?"

It's gotta be her choice.

"Yes." Her tone is sure.

Keeping my grip on her thighs, I spin us around and move down the hall toward my bedroom. Jessa continues to rub herself against me, her bare foot caressing my lower back while keeping us locked together in a tight embrace. It's hard enough to walk with a mammoth erection in your jeans, let alone with the woman of your dreams rocking her hips against you and making it damn near impossible to focus on anything but sliding deep inside her.

I don't know how we make it to the bed, but we do. As I lay her down, she pulls me into her, wrapping her arms around my neck and capturing my lips with hers in a searing kiss. I tug at the zipper of her dress, help her shimmy the garment off her body, and then toss it aside where it lands in a heap next to the bed. She kicks off her remaining shoe and leans down to kiss me.

Her blue eyes sparkle in the lamplight, her cheeks flushed a deep pink as I unabashedly drink in the masterpiece that is her body. I'm awed at the sight of her splayed across my sheets with only the tiny scrap of black cloth nestled low on her hips remaining. Her breasts are full and flushed, her nipples as pink as cotton candy. *And probably just as sweet.*

This woman had the nerve to go on a date with me braless, and I had no goddamn idea.

"You're so sexy," I murmur, leaning down to brush my lips against one peaked nipple.

Jessa arches her back in pleasure, sending the pert flesh between my lips. I swirl my tongue against it, relishing the throaty groan that earns.

"Fuck, Connor . . ."

I nibble softly against the taut skin, letting my eager hands grope and fondle her breasts like I've done in my mind a hundred times before. All those peeks at her cleavage I've shamed myself for . . . and yet I never could have imagined how unbeliev-ably gorgeous her body truly is. Not until now. I release one nipple, moving to the other one while soothing the first with my thumb.

"Oh God." She moans between incoherent gasps, her hips moving up and down as if to tell me *here next, please.*

I'm more than happy to oblige.

I lean back only long enough to pull my shirt

the rest of the way off and lower myself to my knees at the bedside. I pull Jessa down the bed until her quivering legs are draped over my shoulders and her wet, hot panties are just a couple of inches from my lips. The heat emanating from her is making me drowsy with desire. It's almost too much to bear, so I press a chaste kiss to the damp cotton. Hearing her gasp, I look up from between her thighs.

"Can I?" I ask, one finger trailing the slight indentation in the soft fabric where she's most wet.

Her body rolls with pleasure, a whimper trickling from her lips. As soon as the word *yes* reaches my ears, I pull the fabric aside and get to work licking, sucking, and laving at the slick flesh of her core. Jessa quivers with each circle and flick of my tongue, her fingers sliding through my hair as I discover what makes her whimper and what makes her beg.

Just when I feel her beginning to buck with pleasure, I slowly dip one finger inside her, moving until I feel her walls close around me, torrents of raw pleasure washing over her as she sighs my name on the end of a desperate cry.

While she recovers, I spend my time tracing shapes across her thighs with my lips as her hips continue to twitch with the remnants of what I hope was a very good orgasm. Kneeling here, with the smell of her in the air and the taste of her on my lips . . . it's damn near spiritual.

She chuckles breathlessly. "Hey, Connor?"

I grin, nibbling at the plushness of her thigh. "Yeah?"

"You're really good at that."

I laugh. "Thank you."

"I mean it, like, woo." Jessa sighs happily. "Inspiring."

"Oh, really?"

I hope this is going where I think it's going, but I'm not the kind of man to expect some sort of payment in return for a good time. But when she lifts herself onto her elbows and crooks a finger at me, inviting me back onto the bed, I'm not about to object.

Our kisses are slower now, more sensual. I let Jessa guide me onto my back where she straddles me. She still wears her black panties, and I suddenly regret not removing those when I had the chance. What I wouldn't give to have Jessa's entirely naked body perched over mine.

In the lamplight, I catch sight of freckles sprinkling her shoulders and the swell of her breasts, details hidden by shadows until now. *How can someone be this beautiful?*

When I reach for her breasts again, craving their softness, Jessa catches my hands and redirects them to her neck and hair. Slowly, she lowers herself down my chest and abs, marking the trail with electrifying kisses that leave me panting with sexual frustration. I watch as she unbuttons my jeans and pulls down the zipper, yanking my waistband down far enough to release my throbbing erection from my briefs.

Fuck.

"Hold my hair?" she asks, one eyebrow quirking adorably as the soft surface of her palm brushes against the length of me.

I shudder, gently pulling her curls into a riotous ponytail at the back of her neck. With that, Jessa smiles and brushes her lips against my shaft, up and down and back up again until she slides her hot, warm mouth over me in one confident stroke.

"Fuck . . ." I growl, my head falling back on the bed in defeat. "Jessa."

Her lips, tongue, and mouth are so smooth, wet, and tight around me, I can hardly breathe. When one hot little hand palms my balls, I can feel myself *this close* to losing control. Jessa must sense it too because her strokes pick up pace, inching me closer to the edge with each passing second.

"I'm gonna come," I warn her between labored breaths, my heart hammering in my throat. I loosen my grip on her hair as if to say *now's your chance.*

But Jessa doesn't back down. Instead, she pulls me deep into her mouth, swallowing every last drop as pleasure rockets through me.

Holy hell. Now it's my turn to catch my breath.

Jessa climbs up my body and flops to the side of me, both of us taking a moment to recover. Soon, our staggered breaths become low chuckles, and before long, we're both cracking up.

"Why did we wait so long to do that?" Jessa says on a sharp exhale, a wide grin stretching between her flushed cheeks.

"Professionalism, I guess," I say, enjoying the way the bed shakes with our laughter.

Is it too soon to ask her to spend the night?

I don't have time to debate the pros and cons, though, because Jessa is already on her feet and slipping back into her dress. Catching her reflection in the mirror, she groans, pulling her fingers through her tangled hair. She's about to leave, so

I have to milk these final moments before it's too late.

I slide off the bed and pull on my briefs, then pad across the bedroom floor to tug up the long zipper along the side of Jessa's dress. When I finish connecting the tiny clasp at the top, I look into the mirror to see her watching me with a curious expression.

"Why, thank you. You gonna walk me home now too?"

"Of course I am."

I smirk, and Jessa rolls her eyes, her lips quirking into an irresistible little smile. She bends over, grabbing my shirt off the floor and tossing it toward me.

"Then you're going to need a shirt." She winks. "We don't want the neighbors to talk."

Once we're both decent again, I open the very door I had Jessa pressed up against not even an hour ago and lead us outdoors into the night air.

The soft breeze is cool against my skin, which still thrums with the excitement of our post-class extra-curricular activities. Jessa threads her fingers through mine as we cross my lawn and walk up my neighbors' driveway before climbing the stairs that lead to her door.

"Thanks for walking me home." She smiles sweetly, rubbing her thumbs against my knuckles. Just when I think she can't be any cuter, Jessa proves me wrong once again.

"Thank you," I murmur, leaning in, "for a wonderful night."

Under the moonlight and surrounded by the chirping of a thousand cicadas, I kiss her. My hands instinctively rise to cup her cheeks before my fingers thread through her silky hair. She sighs against my lips, pressing against me with a hum of contentment.

When we part, there's nothing more that I want than to ask her to come back home with me and spend the night. But I know better. I don't want to rush her. Maybe the feels that hit me like a ton of bricks are one-sided.

"Good night."

Pressing one final kiss to her forehead, I release her, stepping down the stairs and across the lawn with broad strides. One final glance over my shoulder proves to be worth it. Jessa waves from the landing at the top of the stairs, a soft, secretive grin playing on her lips.

Until next time.

Twelve

CONNOR

It's a beautiful day, so Hayes recommends we take our usual Monday morning Frisky Business meeting outside.

The sun shines brightly overhead, the wind whipping between skyscrapers as we walk toward Grant Park, morning coffees in hand. Car horns and bicycle bells may be irritating to some this early in the morning, but I'm grateful for the background noise. Anything to drown out the incessant questions from Caleb about my weekend.

"Come on, you've got to give me *something*," Caleb says, jogging to my left side so he can meet my pace in stride. "Did you take my advice? Did you go to a class? Please say it was the blow-job one." He grins wickedly.

The bastard.

"Fine," I say, relenting with an eye roll. "I took her to dinner at the bistro and told her about the classes. It was her idea to go, so we did. Let's leave it at that, shall we?"

"Which class?" Hayes turns and walks backward so he can face me, a new sense of interest piqued in him.

"Something spice-related," I mutter, sipping my coffee too soon and burning my tongue. *Fuck.*

"'Spice Up Your Sex Life!'" Caleb says loudly, pumping a fist into the air. "Fuck yeah. How'd it go? Did she get all hot and bothered?"

"Caleb," Wolfie warns from behind us. "Don't be crude."

"That's the goal of the class, isn't it?" Caleb exclaims, seemingly unaware of his own bullshit. "I just want to know. For curriculum-planning purposes."

"The goal of the class is education, you freak," Hayes says with a laugh. "Come on, let's sit. There's a table over there."

He gestures across the grassy expanse toward an unoccupied park table situated under a shady tree. Seems good enough to get to work.

As we all take our seats, Wolfie carefully unpacks our breakfast, a wide array of fresh-baked goods from the local bakery. Soon, I've got an everything bagel positively slathered in chive cream cheese hovering inches from my mouth. But before I can take a bite, I'm confronted with yet another question about Jessa and me.

"How do you think the date went?" Hayes asks, his eyes probing me.

I sigh. Of all the men at this table, he's the one I'd want to talk to the most about this weekend's events. But that doesn't mean I'm going to get into the particulars of my sex life before eight in the morning.

"Really well." I take a bite of my bagel, my teeth making a satisfying crunch into the toasted bread. I'm hungrier than I realized.

"What does that mean? 'Well' could mean anything," Caleb says, unabashedly speaking through a mouthful of orange scone. "'Well' could mean you shook hands and fucked off. 'Well' could mean you went all the way down to bone town. What does that mean?"

"I mean it was a good time."

"Oh shit. You totally fucked." Caleb's eyes double in size, a goofy smile splitting his face as he jumps to his own conclusions. "The nanny broke the drought."

I don't respond, instead taking a sip of coffee that's still not quite cool enough to drink. But I need caffeine if this is how the day's gearing up to be.

Hayes raises his eyebrows at me. "Did you?"

I sigh. Might as well throw them a bone. "Something like that."

Caleb outright howls in triumph and thrusts a fist at me, demanding a knuckle bump. A smile twitches at the corners of my mouth, so I humor him. Gotta admit, the guy's energy is pretty damn contagious.

"Shit, that's great, man," Hayes says, nodding with a sincere look of congratulations in his eyes.

"You don't need to sound so impressed," I grumble. These assholes are acting like I'm some virgin who finally got laid for the very first time.

"I'm just happy for you," he says with a chuckle.

Jackass.

"Okay, gimme the play-by-play. What happened?" Caleb asks, wiping his nose with one finger before planting his elbows on the table and giving me his undivided attention.

All three pairs of eyes are glued on me now, but I don't have a goddamn thing to say.

"It's private," I say, uncomfortable with this amount of attention.

My friends have never been this interested in one of my hookups before. Has it really been that long? Does it matter that much? Or is it because, for the first time, they actually like the girl I'm with?

Caleb leans in, a wicked glimmer in his eyes. "Look, maybe these fucks over here are getting all the ass they could ever want, but me? I'm fucking dying of loneliness. Let me live vicariously through you. I need details."

"No way, man." I laugh, shaking my head. "You won't get anything out of me."

What happened between Jessa and me once that door closed is our business, and no one else's. Not only is it slimy to kiss and tell, but I don't even know how I'd describe our night together.

Mind blowing? Life changing?

I haven't even processed the sheer physical satisfaction of it all, let alone any residual emotions I'm sorting through. All I know is that I like what I have going with her, and I don't want to ruin it by cheapening our memories.

Caleb sighs, hanging his head in defeat. When he looks up again, his brow is furrowed and his eyes narrowed into slits. "Can you at least tell me if it was good?"

"Leave it alone. He doesn't want to talk about it," Wolfie growls out, and I shoot him a grateful glance.

Caleb throws his hands up in surrender. "Fuck, sorry," he says with a sigh, shaking his head. "A year ago, he would've answered the question with a freaking PowerPoint presentation. I just wanna know why this time is different."

That's the big question, isn't it? Why is it different this time? Why is Jessa different?

Is it because it's been so long, and she's like an oasis in the desert? Or is it something about her, about the way she makes me feel, that has me feeling some kind of way? Protective, almost.

The unspoken question hangs unanswered in the air as we all focus our attention on the food. I take a long swig of my coffee before opening my mouth again.

"Jessa is different," I finally say. "I don't know

why, or what that means. There's just something about her that makes me want to be better. She's not some conquest. She's a person I can see myself spending more time with in the future."

I didn't plan on a monologue, but there it is.

The guys stare at me, dumbfounded, and I get it. I'm not usually a romantic. Such sentiments are not in my wheelhouse; all the love affirmations and cutesy bullshit is Hayes's territory. And yet the words don't feel forced or awkward. They feel real. Like I'm telling the truth after weeks of lying to myself.

"Isn't she leaving in, like, a month?"

My head swings around to Hayes, whose question hits harder than I'm sure he intended. All that cream cheese sitting in my belly seems to curdle into stone, sitting in my gut like a boulder.

"Yeah," I mutter, directing my attention back to the coffee in my hands. There's a prolonged silence from the table.

"That sucks, man," Caleb says, his voice uncharacteristically solemn.

Damn right, it does.

I clear my throat. "So, that's that, I guess. When Jessa leaves, I'll be back to square one in more ways than one. Maybe Penelope knows someone in the nanny business."

Wolfie nods. "She's been saying she's gonna give you a call soon."

"Good."

"I can ask Mare too," Hayes says, a thoughtful expression on his face. "Although she told me that Jessa is pretty much irreplaceable."

I couldn't agree more.

Thirteen

JESSA

I t's probably inappropriate to have the thoughts I've been having while holding Connor's baby, but I can't help it.

I can't stop thinking about our date. And I really can't stop thinking about how we spent our time together after the class. Something tells me I'll be thinking about that for a long time.

Marley yawns, her little pink lips forming a perfect circle before settling back into a soft smile. She's nestled against my chest, just a few minutes away from falling asleep.

We've been rocking in the chair next to her crib for the past few minutes, and while Marley's been dozing, there's only been one thing on my mind—Connor's mouth against mine. You'd think the sweet baby smell of Marley's tiny little head would snap me out of it, but nothing's been able to shake the haze of bliss I've been floating around in.

When Marley relaxes in my arms and her little eyes close for good, I stand and place her gently in her crib. Her eyes stay closed, and before she can change her mind about napping, I quietly back out of the room, grateful for a few minutes to myself.

There's something a little sinful about walking around Connor's house without him here. Especially after what we did here the other night. His hands on my body, his length in my mouth.

My belly clenches as I remember it, and a thrill runs down my spine.

He was even more delicious than I'd imagined, in every sense of the word. And standing in his kitchen, a few yards from his bedroom—well, let's just say I've got plenty of ideas about what I'd do if he ever invites me for a round two.

I pull out my phone to find a text from my sister. We've been trying to get ahold of each other for the past few days, and she's asking if I'm free to talk. Settling into the corner of Connor's couch, I dial my sister's number, anxious to hear her voice and tell her all about these new developments.

"Hey, Jess. How's city life treating you?" Taylor's voice is chipper and bright, even through the phone.

She's only a year younger than me, and we've been close since we were kids. Working together to raise your four younger siblings will bond you in ways you didn't think possible, even if she's kind of the yin to my yang. It's only been a little over a week since we last talked, but it feels like we haven't caught up in forever.

"So good, Tay. You have no idea," I say with a low chuckle.

Taylor makes an interested noise, somewhere between a cluck and a chuckle. "You like living above an older couple that much, huh?" she teases.

"Well, I do love how close I am to work."

"Oh yeah, how are things going with the hunky dad? He's not going all pervy on you, is he?"

I know Taylor's just trying to be a good sister, but I can't keep my stomach from sinking a little. This isn't exactly how I wanted this conversation to go.

"Pervy's not how I'd describe it."

"What does that mean?" Taylor's tone is flat, analytical. She's always been the brainy one, needing facts and data.

"He's really sweet, Tay. Like, shockingly sweet. And he's so good with Marley. We've been hanging out, kind of. I mean, I'm friends with his friends now, and they're all super cool. I'm actually starting to feel like I've found my people here."

"Isn't this the guy who owns a sex shop?"

"Co-owns. And they sell adult toys. That doesn't make them monsters. What's wrong with a little pleasure now and then?" I say it as lightly and jokingly as possible, but Taylor only half laughs.

"Right."

"I think you'd really like him, actually," I say. "He's smart like you. And he's got this great sense of humor. He's such an easy guy to be around. I think you two would really get along."

"Why would I meet your boss?"

Her tone isn't accusing or mean, but I can't help feeling like I'm a little in trouble. She may be younger than me, but I swear sometimes Taylor acts like such a big sister.

"We, uh, may or may not have gone on the best first date I've had in my whole life," I say quickly. "And I know what you're going to say, but believe me, it's not what it sounds like. Connor's such a gentleman, and I didn't even realize he was asking me out at first. I think we have a genuine connection. I mean, our chemistry is freaking unbelievable."

I giggle through the last few words, and Taylor clears her throat.

I gulp. Yep, I'm definitely in trouble.

"Jess, don't you think it's a little unwise to start dating someone new? You're about to leave the country for six months."

She's not saying anything I don't already know, but that doesn't change the fact that her words sting like a slap to the face.

I take in a sharp breath and try to ignore the sinking feeling in my stomach. "Yeah, I mean, I know it's complicated, but Connor knows about the trip, and he's cool with it."

"Is that really fair to either of you, though? Are you going to ask him to wait for you? Are you going to wait for him? Who's to say that your soul mate isn't waiting for you in Central America? Do you really want to be too hung up on a single dad to even see it?"

Okay, that doesn't sting. That fucking hurts.

"That's really harsh, Tay."

"I'm not trying to hurt your feelings. I just want you to be realistic, so that you don't get your feelings hurt six and a half months from now."

It feels like my stomach is filled with a giant pile of boulders. I take a deep breath and push away any sadness or anger that's trying to enter my mind.

"Thanks for your concern, but I've got it handled," I say, my voice stiff and a little cold.

Taylor sighs. "Jess, I didn't mean to hurt your feelings. I just want you to be careful, that's all."

"Got the message loud and clear. Hey, I've got to go, Marley's waking up from her nap. I'll talk to you later, okay?"

"Okay. I love you, Jess. I just want what's best for you."

"Mm-hmm. Okay. 'Bye."

I hang up and throw my head back on the sofa. I had a feeling Taylor might be suspicious of Connor, but her fully shutting down any possibility that this will end well? That wasn't what I was expecting.

I check the baby monitor app on my phone to find Marley babbling and waving her arms around. It's time to push my worries about Connor aside and do the job he's paying me for. I'll have to figure out how to feel about all this later.

The rest of the afternoon breezes by. I read a couple of books to Marley before she gets bored and reaches for her toys. I'm just laying her down for tummy time in the living room when I hear the front door unlock, and my stomach lurches.

I guess in all my worrying about Connor, I sort of forgot that I'd actually have to see him at some point today.

Our eyes meet the moment he walks through the door, and it's like everything Taylor said about how I might get hurt just disappears. He flashes me a smile, and it sets off a firework show in my chest. Taylor might be trying to protect me, but she doesn't know him. More importantly, she doesn't know us. And "us" is something I'm dying to learn more about.

"Sorry I'm a little late. I had a meeting that seemed to drag on forever. How was my baby girl today?" he asks, setting his sleek leather briefcase on the counter and joining me on the floor.

This is what I love about Connor. Even in his dress pants and button-down shirt, he doesn't think twice about crouching down on the carpet to play with his daughter. I'd be melting into a sappy sweet puddle if he weren't so damn fun to look at.

I lick my lips and smile down at Marley. "She was an angel, as always. I already fed her. She's just been waiting up for you." *We both have*.

"How about I put her down, and you and I have a glass of wine on the couch. Did you eat? I can whip us up a quick dinner first." Connor picks Marley up and cradles her in his arms. She'll be too big to hold like that soon, and I can tell he's trying to soak up every minute of it.

"You cook?" I stare at him with surprise all over my face. Sometimes he makes it too easy to tease him.

He leans in close to me, so his face is within a foot of mine. I can smell his cologne and practically feel his breath on my skin.

"I can boil water," he says, "and they make really good jarred pasta sauce these days."

I laugh, and the corners of his eyes crinkle. "Pasta sounds delicious."

Connor stands and carries Marley to her bouncy seat near the kitchen, which he straps her into. My heart pounds while I wait for him to finish, and

I decide to put a pot of water on the stove, rather than just stare at his backside.

When he joins me in the kitchen, he arches a playful brow. "I thought I was the one making you dinner."

"You worked hard all day," I say with a shrug. "I figured the least I could do was help."

"You are helping. All the time. Don't pretend like watching Marley isn't hard work. I seriously don't know what I'd do without you."

My stomach drops. I choose not to remind him that I'm leaving in a few short weeks.

Instead, I give him a half smile and shrug again. "All right. Tell me about this jarred pasta sauce."

Conversation flows easily between us as we double-team our dinner. I boil the pasta while Connor pours us some wine. When Marley fusses and wants to be held, Connor frees her from the bouncy seat and holds her with one arm, stirring cooking pasta with the other. I try to pretend that's not totally dreamy.

It's not long before we're sitting on his couch, bowls of spaghetti in hand and wine on the coffee table in front of us. Marley plays with a stuffed pig on the floor.

I realize how silly it might sound, but this is the grown-up life I always pictured for myself. Pasta on the couch with my hubby, and our baby playing nearby . . . it's perfect. A simple life, but one that feels comforting and somehow right.

I let out an involuntary moan when I take the first bite of food. I didn't realize how hungry I was until we started cooking, and Connor wasn't lying about that pasta sauce. I sneak a glance at him to see if he noticed the sound that escaped my throat, but if he did, there's no trace of recognition on his face.

"So," I say between bites, "tell me about this meeting of yours that kept you busy all afternoon."

He shakes his head. "You don't want to know. It was dumb. Number crunching, stuff like that."

"Number crunching sounds important."

"Not this kind. It was one of those meetings that could have easily been an email."

I nod and study Connor's profile, noting the hint of stubble that darkens his jaw. I wonder if kissing him would rub my skin raw. I wonder if his stubble would tickle between my thighs.

Geez. I have to pull it together.

Thankfully, Connor speaks before any other

filthy thoughts can run through my brain.

"How was your day?" he asks. "Besides Marley."

"Fine," I say automatically. Then, after a moment's pause, I add, "I talked to my sister while Marley was napping."

"Where does she fall in the lineup?"

"Number two. She's only a year younger than me. We're close. We were practically inseparable growing up, until about high school when we started competing for everything. But we're good now. It was nice to hear her voice."

"Anything interesting to report?"

I take a sip of wine, studying Connor over the lip of the glass. "I told her about our date, actually. Well, sort of. I guess I just told her about you."

His eyebrows shoot up. "Oh?"

I nod. "She was . . . not as enthusiastic as I'd hoped she'd be."

"Oh."

"Not because of you. You're great. Unbelievably great. I had an amazing time with you, and I made that abundantly clear. She just felt the need to remind me that I'm leaving soon. Central America, six months, blah blah blah."

My gaze drops to my lap. Why am I telling him all this? Suddenly, I don't know why I can't just shut up for once in my life.

"You had an amazing time?"

I look up to find a smile on his face. And not just any smile. *The* smile. The one that only comes out when he's genuinely happy. The one that makes me turn into a useless pile of mush.

I nibble on my bottom lip, unable to speak. All I can do is nod.

"I did too." He rests his arm on the back of the couch, and his fingertips graze my shoulder, sending shivers over my skin. "Let's not worry about the future, okay? Let's just take it one day at a time."

I nod again and turn to face him. Connor reaches out and touches my chin. The gesture is so soft, and yet I can feel his touch deep in my core. I close my eyes, and he takes the bowl from my hands and places it on the table next to his.

"I'm going to kiss you now," he says.

Before I can nod, he's pulling me to him, gentle but firm, and his lips meet the soft skin of my throat. I gasp, and he groans into my neck.

"Never stop making those noises."

Connor traces his tongue over my skin, teasing me. I can't help the sigh that leaves my parted lips, and he tips my head back to expose more of me to him.

Finally, his mouth finds mine and our lips part, tongues tangling. It's only a second before he's pulling back. Marley makes a soft cooing sound from her spot on the blanket at our feet.

"I'd better put her to bed. Can you . . . stick around for a little bit?"

Breathless, I nod.

"Perfect. Wait here."

As he rises and scoops up Marley, I wave and blow her a little kiss. She looks drowsy already. This shouldn't take long.

Connor carries her toward the stairs and then stops and looks over his shoulder at me. "Will you heat her a bottle while I get her into her pajamas and a fresh diaper?"

Knowing that tag-teaming this effort will reduce our time apart, I give him an enthusiastic nod. "How many ounces?"

"Five. And thanks, Jess."

Jess. It's a nickname that's normally reserved for family, but it feels so natural to have Connor use it too.

I get to work while he disappears with Marley upstairs.

In a few minutes, I find them sitting together in her rocking chair. He's cradling her in his arms and whispering sweet words to her. Her eyes are half-closed and she looks so comforted and adored by her daddy, my heart squeezes at the sight of them together.

I tiptoe into the room and hand him the bottle. When he brings it to her lips, she drinks quickly, her eyes now fully closed. We both watch her, enjoying this quiet, sweet moment. And in a few minutes, she's done. When he lifts her, she burps once, and we both chuckle softly as he lays her down in the crib.

As we exit the room together, he takes my hand and gives it a tug. He leads me back to the couch without breaking our connection.

It's quiet between us, and the moment is thick with anticipation. When Connor places a hand behind my neck and urges me closer, I bring my mouth to his once again.

We kiss deeply, quickly picking up right where

we left off before, and soon I'm panting with the need for more.

Suddenly, I realize I'm wearing too many clothes. He's wearing too many clothes. We should fix that.

I reach for the hem of my blouse, but Connor beats me to it, pulling the fabric over my head. He sheds his shirt, baring his chest, and when I reach for him, he pulls me into his lap so I straddle him. With my knees on either side of his hips, I can feel his erection pressing into my thigh. He cradles my head in his hands, his eyes searching my face, scanning me with a fierceness that makes my panties wet.

I don't care if I'm about to leave the country for six months. I don't care what anyone else has to say about it. This is real, and this is right. And more than anything else, I want him.

When he kisses me, it's fast and desperate, like we've been waiting to do this from the moment we met. His hands tangle in my hair, and I grind myself into his lap, causing a strangled groan to pour from his lips. My fingers find the cool metal of his belt buckle. I start to undo it, but he places a hand over mine to stop me.

"Not here," he gasps out.

With one arm firmly wrapped under my ass, Connor stands and starts walking us to his bedroom. I squeal and grasp tightly around his shoulders, placing kisses against the crook of his neck. His cock nudges into my belly with every step he takes, and by the time he closes the door behind us, I'm hungry for more of him. Hungry for a closeness we haven't yet reached.

While I stretch out on his bed, he unbuckles his belt, and I shimmy out of my jeans. Soon, we're both down to our underwear. We lock eyes, and he nods to my bra. I unhook it and toss it in the corner. His gaze moves to my panties. When I slip a finger under the waistband, he stops me, his hands on my hips, kissing my skin as he slowly exposes my center.

"Fuck, you're so wet," he grunts.

I shift my hips, trying to move against him, but he gives me a mischievous grin and turns his face to kiss my inner thigh. I groan in frustration, and he chuckles into me. I want him so badly, it almost hurts. But there's nothing better than the way he teases me.

"Tell me what you want." Connor's voice is firm, commanding, and it makes me want him even more.

I know that once we do this, there's no going back. Our date was one thing, but this? This is different. Serious. Real. Pure, unbridled need. And I've never needed anything more in my life.

"Please," I say softly. "I need you inside me."

Fourteen

CONNOR

The air is humid with the heat of our bodies moving together in perfect time. I can't tell which is driving me crazier—the brush of Jessa's naked skin against mine, or the soft incoherent sighs that fall from her lips when I discover a new sensitive spot to caress with my tongue.

What makes it all the sweeter is that there's no shortage of silky skin to explore and throaty gasps to elicit.

I taste her skin, and she drags her fingernails against my biceps. I bite my lip, a shiver racing down my spine. If I'm not careful, this is going to end a lot sooner than either of us would like.

Sex has never been like this before . . . so tender, like every microsecond matters. I finally know that it's not because I haven't slept with anyone in a while. I remember how that felt compared to this—like seeing the negative of a photo before witnessing the positive in brilliant color. I know now that it's Jessa that makes all the difference. Because when I press forward and sink inside her, it feels an awful lot like coming home.

I rock my hips and she cries out, parting her legs for me and inviting me to sink even deeper. *Goddamn.*

All that cliché nonsense about finding a girl who fits you like a glove? Well, turns out it isn't nonsense after all. Each stroke in and out of her hot, tight pussy feels like trying on my second skin.

I lean down to kiss her lightly on her pink, swollen lips. Her eyes flutter open, finding mine. Emotion crashes through me, and I press my lips to hers in a sweet kiss.

"S-so good," Jessa whispers, her brows knitting together. She reaches up, dragging her fingertips over my cheekbones and stubble.

"I know, baby. I know . . ."

"I want more," she says softly, arching her back just so and prompting my hips with her knees. "Faster. Please."

I obey without another word, quickening my

pace. She throws her head back on the bed with a moan, her hair billowing across the sheets like a crown. I tangle my fingers in it, leaning on one elbow for the leverage I need to drive myself into her. All at once, when my shaft is buried deep within her, she locks me inside, wrapping her legs tightly around my hips.

"Yes, there, yes." She gasps against my mouth, biting down on my lower lip.

Just the sound of her desperation nearly does me in. I pump harder now, giving her exactly what she wants, exactly where she wants it.

It's only a few seconds before Jessa shudders, an orgasm ripping through her from head to toe, trembling around me. The sensation is enough to cut the cord on my own control, and pleasure shoots through me like a goddamn bullet.

This woman is gonna kill me.

As pleasure overtakes me, I gasp out her name. And a second later, I crumple over her in a heap. From beneath me, Jessa breathes deeply, a hearty laugh filling the space where her needy moans were just moments before.

I lift myself onto my elbows to meet her eyes. "Are you crying?"

"I guess I am." She giggles, wiping away a stray tear. "That was intense."

"Good intense? Or bad intense?" My stomach twists in a knot. I sure fucking hope *good intense*, considering I'm still inside her at this point.

"Very good." Jessa nods, and I sigh in relief. "The best kind of good."

"The best, huh?" I give her a smug grin.

"Absolutely," she murmurs happily.

A familiar warmth grows inside my chest, but as much as I'd love to try for round two, I think we both deserve a break. I press a kiss to Jessa's forehead before slowly extracting myself and getting up to dispose of the condom. When I turn back around, she's watching me, lying on her side in a way that displays all her irresistible curves.

I've never been more excited to get back in bed.

Rejoining her, I pull the sheet over our bodies and tuck her against my chest. She nestles into the crook of my shoulder, one arm sliding up my pecs to rest lazily against the side of my neck. Almost in unison, we sigh in contentment. The timing is so good that soon, we're both laughing again.

Goddamn, have I ever laughed with anyone this much?

"Maybe this goes without saying," I murmur against the top of her head with a smile, "but you're invited to stay the night if you want."

"I do want."

She sighs, nuzzling her face into my neck and punctuating the statement with a little nip. I chuckle, tightening my hold on her.

If I could hold her like this always, feeling the steadiness of her heartbeat against my chest, you know damn well that I would. It's so tempting to imagine a world in which I could press PAUSE and preserve this moment for good.

But the reality is that Jessa is leaving me any day now. It's the way it has to be.

It's the last thought I remember before falling asleep, and the first thought I wake up to.

I roll onto my side, blinking away my grogginess as morning light streams in through the window.

Jessa sleeps soundly on the pillow next to mine, her legs pressing against me, the sheet completely thrown aside. The sight of her naked form fills me with an intense yearning. Not just for sex. For her. To be with her. To wake up with her like this every morning.

Get a grip, Connor.

With a sigh, I put more distance between us. I need coffee. And I'm sure she'll appreciate a cup too.

I hoist myself out of bed, shifting the mattress with the idiocy of a bachelor who's accustomed to sleeping alone. Luckily, Jessa is dead to the world, a soft snore reassuring me that she's a deep sleeper and a little noise won't disturb her. The room is cooler now, so I grab a blanket from the end of the bed and gently guide it over her sleeping frame. Then I slip on a pair of basketball shorts and a hoodie and head for the kitchen.

The gurgle and hiss of coffee brewing does nothing to distract me from the brewing of my own thoughts. Just last night, I told her that I'd be down to take things one day at a time. But one day turns into a week, and a week turns into a month, and before long, Jessa is gone and out of my life for God knows how long. The thought is sobering.

Will she want to come back to Chicago after her international adventures? Or will she write me off as a summer fling and jump-start her life somewhere else? Maybe she'll meet someone else while she's away. Someone with a do-gooder heart like hers, and fall desperately in love with him.

The coffee maker beeps quietly, drawing me back to the present where there's a one-of-a-kind woman sleeping in my bed right now. Not in some foreign land, but here with me. And I have to make the most of my time with her before it's too late.

I fill two matching mugs and head back toward the bedroom, softly pushing the door open with my foot. She's now cozied up in the center of my bed, her hair catching hints of sunlight and her cheeks rosy with warmth. I set the mugs on the bedside table, swearing when a drop of scalding liquid leaks onto my thumb.

Caretaker that she is, it's my discomfort that wakes Jessa. Her eyes open immediately, wide with concern. "Are you okay?"

"Yeah." I sigh, annoyed with myself. "I just spilled a little. Careful, it's hot."

She follows my gesture toward the twin cups of coffee, the serious expression on her face melting away into a warm, grateful smile.

"How did you know I take my coffee black?" she asks, cocking her head.

Her tangled hair cascades over one naked shoulder, and it's hard to tear my eyes away from her exposed chest. For as much as I fucking adore her tits, I'm doing an excellent job of maintaining eye contact.

Wait, what did she ask me?

"Truthfully," I manage to say, barely recovering, "I didn't. I take mine black, and it didn't even occur to me to offer you cream or sugar. I actually don't know if I have sugar. I can run to the minimart and grab some if you want—"

Jessa cuts me off, reaching for my hand and giving it a squeeze. "This is great."

I scrub my other hand through my hair, which is officially too long for comfort. "Guess I'm out of practice in this area. The morning-after area."

"Well, that's preferred in my book." She chuckles, leaning in to press a firm kiss against my lips and threading her fingers together behind my neck.

My eyes flutter closed as I relish the simplicity of this domestic moment. And as soon as the pleasure comes, so does its good friend pain.

My heart hitches. *Don't leave.*

When we part, she gives me a sly little smile. "Thanks for the coffee."

Unable to resist, I kiss her again. "You're welcome."

After waiting a bit until it's no longer scalding hot, we both enjoy that first life-giving sip of coffee that comes with the start of each new day. Jessa squirms happily when it reaches her lips, brightening at the flavor.

"God, that's good."

The words throw me back to last night, when she was whispering them in between sexy little whimpers. I feel a kick of interest in my shorts. She looks comfortable as hell, perched up against my pillows without a single swatch of fabric covering her naked body, just the sheet. I'd be lying if I said it wasn't turning me on right now.

"Do you want one of my T-shirts?" I ask, more for myself than for her.

She meets my gaze, drawing the sheets higher up over her chest. "Oh, sure, yeah. Sorry."

Hell no.

Realizing my mistake, I set my coffee down with a soft thunk, not caring if it sloshes onto my nightstand. Planting one knee on the mattress, I lean into her, pulling her cup from her hands and setting it aside before capturing her lips in a hungry, demanding kiss. Jessa sighs against my mouth, her fingers latching onto the thick cotton of my hoodie before wandering beneath to reacquaint herself with the muscles of my torso.

I tug at the sheet, a silent request that she eagerly agrees to. The sheet slides off her shoulders, and before long, I'm mounted between her legs again, grinding myself against her with a desperation that should have been satisfied last night. Seems like Jessa really brings out the sex fiend in me. She opens her lips to the prompting of my tongue, giving me access to the bittersweet taste of coffee already coating her mouth. We both pull back simultaneously, gasping for air.

"You can lie here naked in my bed for as long as you'd like."

"But what if I *want* to wear one of your shirts?" There's that sly smile again.

The image of one of my soft gray tees draped over Jessa's curves flashes through my mind, sending a hot coil of desire down to the now full-blown erection in my shorts.

"Then I'll gladly give you one. But I'd only ask that, eventually, it goes back on the floor where it belongs." I nod down to her perky boobs, which rise and fall with her laughter.

What a sight.

"Don't you have stuff to do today?" she asks before our lips meet again for a brief, sweet kiss.

"Oh yeah. Lots of stuff." I lower myself to her neck, pressing featherlight kisses to her pulse, right where I know she likes it best. "Very important work to do."

"Maybe," she says with a happy sigh, one bare leg lifting to squeeze against my hip, "you should get to work then."

"Whatever you say, boss." I growl into her collarbone before nipping and sucking one perky nipple into my mouth. But when the next words leave Jessa's lips on the tail end of a satisfied sigh, I still.

"I like you a lot, Connor."

It's so frank and sincere that I struggle to find the words to compete. Because how do you tell the woman destined to leave you just how much she means to you?

Well, damn. I guess you just do.

"I like you a lot too, Jessa."

Fifteen

CONNOR

"Hold still!"

Jessa's fingers are splayed across my damp head, turning it this way and that as the foreboding sound of scissors working gets closer and closer to my ears. After putting Marley to bed and popping open a bottle of red, we were ready to cuddle up with a movie and chill for the rest of the night when I caught my reflection in the darkness of the screen.

My hair is longer than it's been in years, so I made the innocent mistake of complaining about it, among a litany of other tedious to-do items I haven't gotten around to yet, like getting my oil changed, updating my voter status, researching new dishwashers. As a single dad with a full-time job and very few free moments to myself, it's hard to summon up the energy to do even the easiest of tasks. So when Jessa offered to trim my hair for me, a job I'd normally assign to a professional, I couldn't think of a good reason to say no.

Now, I can think of a few.

"Remind me how many times you've cut another person's hair?" As hard as I try to mask it, my voice gives away just how nervous I am. I can't go into work looking like I put my head in the blender.

Jessa's eyes meet mine in the bathroom mirror, where I'm fixed like a petrified gargoyle on a stool with a gray towel draped around my shoulders. She goes back to focusing her attention on measuring the hair on either side of my head.

Even in this bright fluorescent lighting, she's beautiful. Watching her at work is always captivating, but having those blue eyes zeroed in on me? It stirs a little excitement in my core. Or maybe that's my nerves, seeing as I might not make it out of this night in one piece.

"Hundreds of times," she says with a confident nod. "Short cuts like yours too. Comes with the territory of being the big sister of a lot of boys who go from buzz cut to Bieber in, like, a week. Why? Are you scared or something?"

"Scared, no. Contemplating my escape? Yes."

Jessa swats me playfully, except she uses the hand with the scissors to do so.

I flinch reflexively. "Cool it, Edward Scissorhands."

"Sorry." She giggles, pressing a kiss to my cheek. "I promise I won't snip you."

"You can snip. Just no buzz cuts."

"Please. You'd look good with or without hair. I'm just going to trim it all down so it's not in your eyes as much. Less bunching up around your ears too. Do you trust me?" Her smile is as contagious as it is calming.

"Yes."

Snip, snip. Snip.

As Jessa begins to shape the mop on my head, I close my eyes, focusing on the sensation of her fingertips combing through my damp hair. It's a comforting feeling, knowing you're in good hands. And Jessa's hands have a magical, soothing effect on me. I'm beginning to doze when her voice draws me back.

"You just have the one sibling, right?"

I blink open my eyes lazily. "Yeah, it's just me and Penelope."

"She's really nice. I like her. It's a relief, honestly—she treats me like she's known me longer than six weeks."

"That's my sister for you. All she wants is for everyone within a mile radius of her to be happy. She's kind of a people pleaser in that way."

Using two fingers, Jessa lines up a few uneven strands along the side of my head and straightens them with a single confident snip. "Is that a bad thing?"

"No," I murmur, shrugging, and Jessa gives me a warning look as if to say *didn't I ask you to sit still?* Must be the big sister in her coming out. "Not with Wolfie there to look out for her and make sure she's taking care of herself too. How about you? What are your siblings like?"

"Oh wow, where to begin? There are six of us, to start."

"Geez. Six." My eyes widen. "That must have been a lot."

"Mm-hmm. Three girls and three boys. Me and Taylor and my little brother are my mom's kids from her first marriage. The twins and little Cara are from her second marriage."

I sense there's a story there that Jessa isn't telling me. But as curious as I am, I ultimately make the call not to pry. If she wants to tell me, she will.

"That's quite the family."

She quirks an eyebrow and lets out a humorless laugh. "No kidding. I love them all to death, don't get me wrong, even when they're being total assholes. But when I was at home, it was like . . . I don't know."

She shakes her head, her mouth twisted into a frown. "I couldn't be myself. I was too busy making sure that no one was eating glue or stepping into traffic. Money was really tight for a while there, so my mom and stepdad were working full-time jobs at all sorts of odd hours to pay for, well, the six kids between them. So there was an unspoken expectation that I was the backup plan, the perpetual babysitter."

"That must have been really hard."

She smiles, relief written all over her features. "You can imagine how nice it was to leave and go to college. Coming home for the summers to help with the kids wasn't a walk in the park exactly, but it beat being on call twenty-four/seven. Can you tip your chin down?"

I do as she asks, feeling her warm fingers brush against the back of my neck. "Sounds like you've always been working, even at home."

Jessa snorts. "Yeah, I guess you're right. Although, it's been nice renting from the Wilkeses, making a little home for myself. Did you know their son is coming home from his shore-duty tour early?"

"I didn't. What does that mean for you?"

Her voice turns solemn. Thoughtful. "Well, he needs somewhere to stay, so my lease is ending a few days early. They're being super fair about it, though. I mean, they cut my rent in half this month, so I'm really the one winning here."

I frown. "But . . . where will you stay? Your trip isn't for another two weeks. Are you leaving early?"

"Chin up," Jessa says.

At first I think she's caught on to the quiet stress underlying my casual tone. Then I remember where we are and what we're doing. I lift my chin, and Jessa drags her fingers over my forehead, combing the wet hair back.

"Thank you."

Snip, snip. Snip, snip.

Finally, she answers my question. "I can't leave

early because my flight is already booked. So you don't have to worry about finding an interim nanny between me and whoever you've got lined up to take over next month."

The truth is, I have no one lined up. Because contracting another nanny means that I have to accept the fact that Jessa is really leaving.

While I do understand that, in theory, I've been avoiding processing it fully. The truth is, I've been dreading replacing Jessa. Even more so, I've been dreading losing Jessa. My stomach tightens with dread at the thought.

"However," she says, snapping me out of my sad spiral, "I do need a place to stay for the last few days. I was thinking about asking Scarlett if I could crash in her guest room. How much do you think is fair to offer her?"

I ignore Jessa's question, instead asking one of my own, barely formed before it barrels out of my mouth. "Why don't you just stay here?"

Her hands still in my hair, a look of surprise plastered on her face, she watches me, waiting for some sort of punch line. But it isn't a joke. Although, if she doesn't respond soon, I'll have to force myself to play it off as one.

"You don't mean that." She laughs, shaking her

head. "You're only saying that because I've practically got a blade to your neck." She emphasizes the word *blade* by snipping once again with the scissors.

I swallow, steadying my voice to sound as casual as I can without seeming flippant. "I mean it. We're nearing the end of the second quarter at Frisky Business, and I still have to meet my quota. Meaning I'm only going to get busier until then. I could use your help taking care of Marley at night too."

"Your quota?" Jessa narrows her eyes, all skepticism and uncertainty.

"Yep." It's not a lie. Not really. I do have to meet a quota of customer interactions that yield goods sold.

But I'm not going to tell her that I'm only two points away from my goal, a milestone I'm sure to pass tomorrow. And I'm certainly not going to tell her that the reason I want her to move in has little to do with Marley at all. Because that would require me admitting to myself that I'm in love with my baby girl's nanny.

Oh fuck.

Jessa mulls over my offer while my thoughts stop dead in their circular tracks, focusing on one simple fact, as clear as a summer sky.

I love Jessa McClaine.

I love this gorgeous, contemplative woman. I love her eyes. I love her freckles. I love the way she snorts a little when she laughs. I love the feel of her fingertips trailing across my skin. I love how she smells, how she tastes, how she makes me feel when she meets my eyes across a room. I love how she loves my daughter, how she looks so at home, so at peace, holding Marley in her arms. I love Jessa and all the complications that come with her.

Well. Isn't that the most tragic thing you've ever heard?

"I guess it would make the commute easier, not that it was ever much of a hike." She laughs, though her voice is a bit uneasy. "Are you sure?"

The question is honest. Practical. Giving me a way out. Little does she know that I'm already trapped.

I do my best to crack a smile. "As long as you don't totally butcher this haircut, you can move in as soon as we're done here."

Jessa scoffs but a grin sneaks across her lips, the kind of grin I'm desperate to kiss. "I'm already done, you diva. What do you think?"

I really haven't been paying attention to the haircut, I guess. I've been lost in thought, so I take this opportunity to ground myself in the present.

With the sides and back cut down several inches and plenty of length remaining on top to play with, Jessa's gone and given me a near-professional cut. I'm honestly kind of impressed by the sharp yet roguish man I find in the mirror.

"Not bad." I smirk, running a hand through the almost dry hair. *Damn, that feels better.*

"Not bad?" She guffaws. "Seriously? This is the best haircut I've ever given, thank you very much."

I chuckle, grabbing one of her hands and pulling it to my lips to plant a firm kiss on her knuckles. "It does look good. Thank you. I love it."

"Really?" Jessa asks, that innocent streak shining through all the sass and snark. "You do?"

"Yeah," I murmur against her fingers.

I spin around on the stool, looping my arms under her knees and hoisting her onto my lap. Her startled gasp quickly dissolves into a fit of giggles as I run my hands up and down the smooth fabric of her leggings, peppering tiny kisses on her neck and collarbones.

"You never answered my question," I growl into her ear, flicking my tongue against the soft skin just behind it.

She sighs, wrapping her arms around my neck and scooting herself closer into my groin, which is already hardening in record time. My hands find her ass, giving it a good, hard squeeze that earns me a heady moan of approval.

"Which question was that?" she asks, her voice already trembling with desire.

God, I love the way this woman makes me feel, nearly as much as I love the way I make *her* feel. I trail my fingers up her loose-fitting tee, wandering the expanse of her back and shoulders until finding the thick strap of her sports bra and giving it a needy pull.

"Will you move in with me?"

I pull the sports bra down Jessa's shoulders with a firm tug before capturing her tits in my hands and pinching her nipples between my fingers. She grinds herself into my lap, one hand braced against the bathroom sink for support, the other playing with my fresh haircut.

"Yes, as soon as they need the room back." She groans before continuing with a steadier voice. "On one condition."

"What's that?"

"We take a shower, immediately." She chuckles, leaning back to look me in the eye. "Don't you feel all the tiny hairs on your neck and shoulders? You're absolutely covered."

I shrug with a lazy smirk, giving her nipples another pinch, and Jessa gasps, her eyes never leaving mine as her cheeks flush a darker shade of pink. "I'm pretty focused on feeling other things right now."

"Well," she murmurs, leaning in to brush my lips with hers. Her tongue slides teasingly across my lower lip. "I also have all your damn little hairs on me, and I'm really itchy."

I glide my hand behind the back of her slight neck, pulling her mouth to mine for a greedy, sloppy kiss. I lean back, our lips separating with a wet pop. "I guess it's shower time then."

With that, I stand, carrying Jessa with me, and open the shower curtain. When I crank the shower knob, she shrieks before clapping a hand over her mouth so she doesn't wake the baby. In the steamy shower, we peel off our clothes and collide again in a desperate embrace, this time fully naked with nothing left to hide.

But with my little revelation this evening, I am

hiding something, aren't I? It's all I can think about when I have her pinned against the tile wall, thrusting with her legs locked like a vice around my hips.

It takes everything in me not to blurt it out in rhythm with the sound of her chanting my name as we lose ourselves to a tidal wave of pleasure that leaves us both gasping for air.

I love you.

I love you.

I love you.

Sixteen

JESSA

My flight is only days away, and it feels like I've eaten a three-course meal consisting entirely of rocks. I've never been so reluctant to get on a plane in my entire life.

Leaving Chicago now, after the friends I've made, the people I've met, after Connor? Suddenly, this trip feels insane. Like something someone does when they don't have anyone or anything. I'm different now. I'm not who I was when I signed up to go. I have people, people who want me here, people who need me.

And goddammit, I need them too.

I've already thought through every possible escape route to get out of this trip, but there's no way. I signed all kinds of waivers and contracts when I signed up. Hell, there was a rigorous application process to get in. This isn't one of those eat, pray, love things. I agreed to go and help people, and that's exactly what I have to do. There's little choice. Even if every minute spent away from Connor and Marley will break my heart into smaller, more jagged pieces.

God, just the thought of it causes an actual pain inside my chest. It's not as though I'm going away on vacation. I'll be gone for months and months. Connor is an amazing catch—of course he'll have found someone else by the time I return. I'll have lost my shot with him forever.

My phone dings, and a notification flashes on the screen.

PACK!

Ugh. It's a reminder I set for myself a couple of hours ago, when I felt this dread about leaving creeping over me. So I set the reminder and sprawled out on my bed in my little apartment, letting myself wallow for a bit. I've got to get packed so I can move over to Connor's place for the next few days anyway. And *that* is something I'm definitely looking forward to.

It's taken all kinds of willpower not to scroll through pictures of Marley and me on my phone, or through pictures of Connor on his Instagram.

There's only one place that kind of sentimentality will lead, and it's not anywhere I want to be right now. Not if I can help it. I can't go there right now, because if I do, I'll cry. And I have too much to get done to dissolve into tears.

I force myself to sit up, and then I drag my old suitcase down from the shelf in my closet. And a duffel bag. And another suitcase. And a weekend bag, just to be safe. Since I started working for Connor, I've put off even thinking about packing, and now I have to figure out how to fit everything I own in two suitcases. Before I left Indiana, I gave away or donated everything I could live without, but I still have too much to take with me on this international trip.

I take a deep breath, push my sadness aside, and start digging through my closet.

Is four bags too much for a mission trip where I'm supposed to be spending my time serving others? I know that everyone always says to travel light, but it's not like I'm packing my bags full of makeup or hair products. I just can't think of anything I'm ready to leave behind.

Like, I'm pretty sure I'm going to need a few different pairs of jeans, and all my fun tops, and some basic T-shirts, and obviously every pair of shorts I own. And it only makes sense to pack some dresses too, right? It's not like I'll only be working all the time.

So that means that I need to bring some cute shoes, maybe a pair of wedges, and those strappy sandals I've been wearing all summer. The same ones I wore on my first date with Connor, which, let's be real, still stands as the hottest date I've ever been on in my life. And if I'm bringing the strappy sandals, I should probably bring some comfortable shoes too, like the sneakers I wear when I take Marley on a walk around the neighborhood.

Gah! And we're back to Connor and Marley.

I used to be so excited for this trip. This was the only thing I was looking forward to for so long, and now? Now the thought of leaving makes me sick to my stomach.

I toss the sneakers I was holding onto the floor and throw myself back onto the bed, burying my face in my hands. I haven't felt this torn up about something in . . . well, I don't know how long. My heart hurts. Like, physically hurts. I don't know how I'm going to walk onto that plane without puking my guts up or bawling my eyes out.

Even the thought of all the good we'll be doing over there isn't doing anything to comfort me. Because I have people who need me here too. Connor needs me, and so does Marley. And leaving them now just feels so freaking wrong.

My phone buzzes again, only this time it doesn't stop.

I roll over and pick it up to find a number I don't recognize calling me. But I do recognize the area code. It's the same as the area code of the phone number of the agency that's organizing the trip. Probably some last-minute check-in that I've gotten all my immunizations and have my passport up to date. That kind of routine stuff.

"Hello?" My voice is raspier than I thought it would be. And I haven't even started crying yet.

"Hi, is this Jessa McClaine?" It's a woman's voice. She's chipper and professional, the kind of person who likes to help people. The kind of person who goes on these trips without a second thought.

"Speaking."

"Hi, Jessa, this is Cassidy. I'm calling about your upcoming trip. Do you have a minute?"

"Yep, I'm all ears. I was just packing, actually."

"Oh, well, you might want to put a pause on the packing. We have a proposal for you. It's a little out of left field, so don't feel pressured to say yes, but we could really use you in a different area of the organization."

My stomach falls to my feet. I nod, and then I remember that she can't see me. "I see. What's the proposal?"

"So, I know you had your heart set on traveling abroad, and I know this is very last minute, but we're actually very much in need of volunteers here in the States. You're in Chicago, correct?"

"Correct," I blurt out faster than she can finish her sentence.

"Okay, that's what I thought," she says with a chuckle. "So, yeah, we've just received a call that we have eighty-five refugees on their way to Chicago from El Salvador and Honduras. We need a few of our staff members to stay behind and help coordinate these people's next moves. Now, it's going to be a big job. They'll need a lot of support finding housing, employment, childcare. The kids will need to be enrolled in local schools, doctor's appointments, vaccines. We've already got two verbal commitments, but we're looking for one more person to give up their spot on the trip to help with this project. Is this something that you'd be interested in?"

My mind is spinning from all the information she just gave me, but one thing stands out above all the rest of the noise.

I don't have to leave anymore. I can stay here. I can stay with Connor and Marley.

I almost sob with relief. Thankfully, I take a moment to compose myself.

"Jessa?" she asks.

"I'm here," I say, quickly doing some mental gymnastics to see if making this compromise on staying here to work for the organization will mean losing a piece of myself. I do want to have a real shot with Connor, but I want to be sure I'm considering all sides. I don't want to give up on my dreams.

Cassidy clears her throat. "If you need to think about it . . ."

"I don't. I would love to stay and help with this project."

The words feel like they're being spoken by someone else, but it's my voice that's delivering them. My brain's still not quite able to process the full reality of what's happening right now, but I know it's what I truly want.

Cassidy barrels forward like it's the most natural thing in the world. "That's great news, Jessa. Thank you so much for your generosity and willingness to step up where you're needed. Your verbal commitment will be satisfactory for now, but we'll send a written contract in the mail, and you should receive it next week."

"Okay. That sounds fine."

"Awesome. We'll be in touch with more information soon, but before I let you go, do you have any questions for me at this time?"

"Um, thank you? I mean, I just really appreciate this opportunity."

Cassidy laughs. "You're welcome. We'll be reaching out to you soon about start dates and any additional paperwork we'll need you to fill out."

"Okay. Thank you. 'Bye."

I hang up and sit there with the phone in my hand for what feels like another five minutes.

Do I have some kind of supernatural power I'm not aware of? Or maybe I've got some kind of super-special connection to God or whoever's in charge up there. Whatever it is, I'm going to need a minute to process what the hell just happened.

I'm not leaving anymore.

I'm staying here.

I'm staying here in Chicago, and that means

Connor and I can be together.

Holy shit.

The full weight of the reality of what's happening hits me all at once, and I jump up from the bed and punch my fists in the air. In any other circumstance, it would feel corny as hell, but right now, I don't know what else to do. There's no other way to express how freaking over the moon I'm feeling right now.

Actually, that's not true. I can think of plenty of things I'd like to do the next time I see Connor. And the best part is, the next time I see him definitely won't be the last.

Relief rushes through me, and I fall back onto the bed with a huge grin on my face.

Seventeen

CONNOR

This is hopeless.

After scrolling through another nanny's résumé and references, I press the heels of my hands against my tired eyes.

I haven't been sleeping well, knowing that Jessa is just days away from disappearing from our lives like she was never here in the first place. And it isn't just the task of finding another nanny that's overwhelming me. It's the idea that I may lose my one shot at something truly promising.

If I lose Jessa, I know I could lose more than just a chance at a relationship—I could lose a chance at real happiness.

I click to open another application with a sigh. Plenty of experience, two glowing referrals, a holistic approach to childcare . . . everything a single dad could want in a nanny.

I turn to Marley, who's been busying herself in the bouncer at my feet by gnawing on a teething toy. It's pretty much impossible not to pause and marvel at how big she's already gotten in just a handful of months. I wonder if she'll remember Jessa, her loving caretaker for these crucial months of development, or if she simply won't notice the swap of one pair of warm arms for another.

I lower my laptop to her level so she can get a good look at the applicant's résumé. "What do you think? Does she seem like your type?"

Marley looks at the screen. Frowning, she flaps her pudgy little arms as an animated squeal leaves her lips.

"Yeah, me neither."

It takes the rest of the afternoon, but I've narrowed it down to three potentials. One older nanny with experience as an au pair abroad, one younger nanny with a graduate degree in child development and psychology, and one last nanny with an address conveniently near mine. To calm Marley's fussing, I've long since tucked her against my chest, and she's now snoring softly into the worn fabric of my shirt.

I'm just beginning to doze too when I'm roused by a soft knock at the front door.

Jessa?

That can't be right. She should be downtown at the nonprofit's headquarters, finalizing the paperwork for her trip. And if she isn't downtown, she'd certainly be busy packing away what few belongings she has upstairs at the Wilkeses'.

Maybe she has to leave early and she came to say good-bye. Or maybe it's just one of the census people again.

I take a deep breath, and with Marley in one arm, somehow manage to get myself up from the couch without waking her. And when I open the front door, any uncertainty I had about things between Jessa and me collapses into a warm puddle of all the sappy emotions, all at once.

Jessa stands on my front porch, a warm smile on her lips. "Hi," she says breathlessly.

I drink in the sight of her—the casual tee, the comfortable leggings, the familiar sneakers—and I nearly choke on the lump camping out in my throat. *Don't leave.*

"Hey," I manage to croak out. "What's up? I thought you were doing trip stuff today."

"I was." She nods, breaking eye contact with me to stare at her shoes. "And then I got a call." She twists her fingers together, a nervous gesture.

I arch an eyebrow. "What about? Is everything okay?"

"Well, it's a lot to explain."

"Okay. Do you want to come inside?" I nod my head toward the ajar door, careful not to jostle the sleeping baby nestled peacefully against my chest.

"It's so nice out. Can we talk out here?"

Does she not want to come in? My body tenses on instinct. *What the hell is going on?*

"Of course."

I step inside briefly to grab a blanket to keep Marley warm against the beginning of a breeze that feels more like fall. Soon, the three of us are sitting together on the front porch, watching the sun set over the tall trees lining my street.

I turn to see a contemplative look on Jessa's face. I'm impatient, but I train my voice to be gentle. "Jessa, tell me what's going on."

"So, here's the thing. I got offered a job. Not the abroad job . . . um, one here in Chicago. It's with the same nonprofit organization, but it turns out they need more support here in Chicago than they do in El Salvador. So they've offered me a position here."

Oh. My heart is pounding at the base of my throat, a triumphant cheer desperate to be released. But I keep my mouth shut. Better to keep my hopes low and not set myself up for more hurt. But still, I can't help thinking . . . *don't leave.*

"And I said yes."

The cheer dissolves into a strangled sigh, deflating all my tension and stress and leaving nothing but pure relief. *Thank fuck.*

I lean into Jessa, resting my forehead on her shoulder. She giggles, leaning her head on mine.

"I'm so glad," I whisper, tightening my hold on Marley. "She will be too, once she wakes up."

"Which could be at any second, if I know anything about this little girl," Jessa says with a laugh.

"And you most certainly do." Which is why it's been so hard to find a replacement. I lift my gaze to hers, enjoying the way the setting sun colors her cheekbones a dusty pink. "Why the hell did you lead in like you were sharing bad news?"

She chuckles. "I don't know. I guess I was worried this would change things between us. I've been gearing up to leave for, like, *months*, and suddenly I'm staying? I didn't know how you'd feel about that."

I reach out to cup the side of her face, drawing my thumb across the softness of her cheek. "I feel happy. Happier than you could ever imagine."

A smile flickers across Jessa's lips before settling into a soft frown.

"But you still have to find a new nanny," she says, concern in her eyes. "With this new job, I'll be working full time, plus probably overtime when it's needed. I wish I could, but I can't be in two places at once."

"Don't worry about that. I've already got three good options picked out." Suddenly, I'm very glad I did all that tiresome work today. I can see the weight lifting off of Jessa's shoulders as she sits up a little straighter.

"Really?"

"Really."

A shadow of disappointment falls over her features. "I'm going to miss taking care of Marley." Her eyes meet mine with a desperation I know all too well. "Not just Marley. I'm going to miss you too. But staying in Chicago means I need to find a new apartment—"

"Move in with me."

She sighs softly, turning away with a scoff and shaking her head slowly. "No, Connor. You've been kind enough already, offering to let me stay here for a few days."

"I'm not being that kind. I'm actually being incredibly selfish."

"Come on . . ."

"Jessa, I mean it. Move in with me. With us. Permanently."

She blinks, turning back toward me with a curious look in those big blue eyes. "Permanently?"

With the hand not securing Marley, I take Jessa's fingers and bring them to my mouth to brush whisper-soft kisses against her knuckles.

"Jessa . . . this is all new to me. I haven't felt the way I feel about you with anyone else. You could be leaving for El Salvador as planned, and I'd still feel the same damn way. But you're not leaving, and maybe that makes me greedy, because I don't want to let you go. I don't want to spend a single day away from you. So, please, move in with me. With us." I meet her eyes, the blue orbs filling with tears. "I don't want you to let me go either. I don't want to let you go."

Tears fall freely down her freckled cheeks now, so I capture them with tender kisses. And when her lips meet mine in a passionate, gasping kiss, all that matters is the touch of her skin against mine.

We part only when my daughter, now predictably wide awake, begins pulling at Jessa's hair. While we attempt to pry a tiny fistful of curly locks from Marley, she laughs gleefully, a laugh so contagious we can't help but join in.

Jessa leans down to plant an adoring kiss to my baby girl's forehead, and I press my lips to the crown of Jessa's head, sharing one of many priceless moments to come.

I'm certain of it.

Eighteen

JESSA

Let's just say this isn't how I expected my summer to go. Today couldn't be more perfect. Connor at the grill, Marley in my arms, all our closest friends laughing and eating in our backyard.

That's right. *Our* backyard. I'm still not quite over that one yet. It's a big upgrade, going from renting out a room in someone else's house to sharing a home with the man you adore. I'm not quite over that part of all this either. How perfectly everything's worked out with Connor. Some things in life are just fate, I guess.

"She's getting bigger every day, isn't she?" Scarlett scrunches her nose and coos at Marley, who smiles back at her.

Penelope, Scarlett, Maren, and I are huddled in a circle on the deck, drinking rosé and admiring the men from afar. I'll be honest, I appreciate my new friends even more now that I almost left them all for Central America. We were just starting to get close right before I was about to leave, and I feel so lucky to have this time with them to gossip and giggle and talk about life.

I nod and kiss the top of Marley's head. "She'll be wearing clothes for six-month-olds in no time," I murmur, shaking my head. "I wish there was a way to make time stop, just for a little while."

"Well, it sounds like you kind of figured that one out. Weren't you supposed to be in El Salvador like, yesterday?" Scarlett asks with a sly, questioning grin.

"Yeah," Penelope says, crossing her legs and nodding toward me. "Connor gave me the basics, but I feel like we need the whole story from you."

My lips curl into a half smile, and I shrug. "A new position opened up here in the city, and they needed someone to stay behind to fill it. I jumped at the chance, really. If you'd asked me a few months ago, I would have told you I was ready for a big change like moving to Central America. Turns out that big change was something else entirely."

My gaze wanders across the yard to Connor, who's laughing, the heat from the grill making him appear to shimmer. His eyes meet mine and his smile softens a little, sending my stomach into a series of backflips.

I really am a lucky girl.

"You two are adorable," Maren says, nudging my side with her elbow.

I can feel a blush warming my cheeks. "Thanks. It's fast, I know, but trust me. It's more real than anything I've ever felt before."

"I know what you mean," Penelope says, giving me a smile that reminds me a lot of her brother. "I'm really happy for you both."

Scarlett sighs and claps her hands together loudly. "All right," she says, rising from her seat. "As thrilled as I am for the new lovebirds—and don't get me wrong, I really am happy for you, Jess—I'm starving. Please tell me the boys are done with those burgers already."

She couldn't have spoken too soon. The men clamber up onto the deck, teasing each other and roughhousing like always, with Connor herding them up the steps, a platter full of cooked meat in his hands.

"I hope you ladies came ready to eat," Connor says. "Come on into the kitchen. We've got it all set up in there."

Everyone files into the house, and I hang back to wait for Connor. He sees me waiting and slips an arm around my waist, kissing the top of my head.

"How's my little girl doing? Time for a change?" he asks, nodding to Marley.

"I think she's okay. We should eat first, then I can change her."

He nods again and pulls me closer to his side. "I like this. Having you here all the time. Hosting with you. Getting to make eyes at you across the yard whenever I want."

His voice is low, possessive, and impossibly sexy. Suddenly, my skin feels electric under his touch.

"I like this too," I say, my eyes searching his face. "But I'd be lying if I said I wasn't looking forward to when everyone's gone."

His mouth goes slack for a second before twisting into a devilish smile. "You'd better get inside before I do something to make them all leave early." He leans in and kisses my neck, quick and hot, in just the right place to make me let out a small gasp.

This man will be the death of me.

Connor and I walk inside to find our friends gathered in the kitchen, putting plates of food together and talking loudly about the latest customer horror story from the store.

"And I tried to explain to her as nicely as I could that we don't accept returns at Frisky Business," Caleb says, a mischievous glint in his eye. "But this woman just wouldn't take no for an answer."

Scarlett shrugs. "So she's a woman with strong convictions."

Caleb stares at her incredulously. "It was a used dildo, Scar. There's no way I was taking that thing back."

"Okay, can we change the topic, please? Some of us are trying to eat," Maren says, shooting daggers across the room at Caleb.

When Caleb raises his hands in apology, Hayes shoots him a pointed look. "Maybe a slightly more dinner-friendly topic?"

"How's the new job, Jessa?" Wolfie asks between bites of his burger.

"It's still early yet, but so far, so good," I say.

Connor takes Marley out of my hands so I can make myself a plate of food. "They're lucky to have her," he says, "and so are we."

The girls all sing "awww" in unison, while the boys, I'm sure, are just tucking that sappy comment away to tease Connor about later. They really do like to rib each other like brothers.

We fill in the crew on the new nanny we hired for Marley. She's in her fifties with four grown children and a grandbaby on the way, and seems to be a perfect fit so far.

After we finish eating, everyone hangs out in the living room to chat for a while before the couples pair off and head home for the night. Connor puts Marley down, and I slip off to the bedroom, where I've got a little surprise planned for him.

Marley was pretty tired by the time everyone left, so I know I've only got ten minutes tops before Connor joins me in here, and I have to move fast. I slide my sundress over my shoulders and slip into the black lace bra and panty set I bought last weekend, complete with a skimpy, see-through, knee-length robe that I leave untied and open. I can hear Connor walking down the hallway, so I run my fingers through my hair and perch myself on the edge of the bed, one leg crossed over the other.

When Connor steps through the door and lays eyes on me, he stops dead in his tracks. Raw lust washes over his face, and his gaze roams hungrily over my body.

"Hi, there," I say, uncrossing and recrossing my legs.

"Hi," he says, his voice a low growl. He walks toward me, his eyes still trained on my body.

"Did Marley go down okay?"

"Mm-hmm. She's fine," he says absently, like sleeping babies are the very last thing on his mind.

"Good. So, I was thinking . . ." I let my voice trail off as I play with the tie of my robe.

Connor's gaze meets mine, his eyes on fire. "Yeah?"

"Remember our first date? All that stuff about accelerators and brakes?"

He chuckles. "It'd be pretty hard to forget."

"Well, is your engine revving yet?"

With a mischievous look, he pulls me to my feet to fully admire the lingerie. His hands trail over my skin, sending chills down my spine. In that class on our first official date, we'd both indicated lingerie was an accelerator.

He wraps an arm around my waist and pulls me to him, kissing me hard but slow, like he's drinking me in. When we part, he brings his lips to my ear and murmurs, "My engine's been revving since you decided to talk dirty on the deck just out of earshot of our friends. But yeah, it's definitely heated."

I slip the robe off my shoulders as Connor tugs his T-shirt over his head. Then he just admires me, running his big palms along my sides. I press up on my toes to briefly kiss his lips.

He sheds his jeans and kicks them into the corner, then pulls me onto his lap on the bed. We kiss again, more urgently this time, my knees on either side of his hips, and I can feel his bulge pressing into my belly.

The need I have for him is insatiable, like no matter how many times I feel his body pressing into mine, I'll always want more. More of him, more of this, more of *us*.

He brings his lips to the tender skin above my breast, kissing and sucking gently as his fingers fiddle with the clasp of my bra.

"Can I help you with that?" I ask, a slight tease in my voice.

He nips gently at my skin and growls, brushing his tongue over my nipple. Even through the lace, the sensation sends a shock to my core.

The hook of my bra unclasps, and Connor groans in triumph. As I toss it to the floor, he takes my nipple in his mouth, rolling it under his tongue. I grind down into him in response, and he groans again, but this time it comes from somewhere deeper and darker inside him.

"Do you remember what else we talked about that night?" I ask between breaths.

He looks up at me and nods, his cock twitching in his briefs. "We talked about a lot of things."

"Anything you want to do, I'm game."

His eyebrows rise. "Anything?"

I nod. "I said I like to try new positions, didn't I?"

His lips curl into a smile, and he presses his face into my chest. "You're going to be the death of me, you know that?"

I shrug and nibble at his ear. "There are worse ways to go."

Connor laughs, his breath hot against my skin. He kisses my neck and lies back on the bed, spinning me around and dragging my hips toward him until I'm aligned over his face.

This is something I've been thinking about nonstop since it came up in the game of *yes or no*, and I'm relieved that this is his choice. I wasn't lying when I said I was game for anything, but the two of us pleasuring each other at the same time has been at the top of my to-do list for weeks now.

He presses his lips to the dampness of my panties. I moan and arch my back, holding on to his hips for stability. Okay, this is going to take a lot more focus than I thought.

"Fuck, babe, you're so wet," he murmurs.

I pull at the elastic of his briefs until his cock springs free. God, I've missed this. Since I moved in, we haven't been able to keep our hands off each other, and still, none of it ever feels like enough.

He pushes my panties to the side and kisses my center just as I take his length in my mouth. We groan simultaneously. It's magic.

Raw need pulses between us, and the pleasure is almost blinding.

Connor murmurs sweet and dirty things into my flesh between swipes of his tongue. How good I taste, how much he adores me, how happy he is. My heart is filled with emotion, and my body sings with pleasure. I never imagined being so worshipped and happy. It's almost disorienting.

And this is only the beginning . . .

Nineteen

JESSA

Six months later

"All right, kid, here's the sitch."

With a little extra effort, I kneel down to Marley's level on the foam play mat. It's not easy in my figure-hugging date-night dress and heels that still need some breaking into.

Marley's big blue eyes peek out from under her dark curls and find mine despite her latest obsession—actively gnawing on the ear of a new bunny friend, courtesy of Uncle Hayes. At this age, she's always got something in her mouth.

"Aunt Penny and Uncle Wolfie are coming by soon. They're gonna watch you while your daddy and I go on a date. Remember Aunt Penny and Uncle Wolfie?"

Marley gurgles, smacking her wet lips together until she . . . makes a dolphin sound? Unclear.

"Eeooo!"

Yep, that's definitely a dolphin sound.

I laugh, shaking my head in disbelief. "Yes, that's right. Uncle Wolfie is coming."

"Eeoooooo!"

"That's her saying 'Wolfie'?"

I turn to find Connor standing over us, fastening the cuff links on his crisp white button-up.

Well, hot damn. He's looking all kinds of fine in his date-night suit, a sharp gray number that makes his green eyes pop like freaking traffic lights and ignites my libido into overdrive.

"How long has she been barking?" He holds out a hand to me and pulls me to my feet.

"Honestly, I have no idea. And I thought it was more like a dolphin," I say with a sigh as Connor chuckles and gazes down at Marley with adoration. "Scarlett and Mare hogged her the whole time at the Christmas party, and I can see them planting that seed."

Connor laughs, a sound that reverberates straight through my core and down to my toes.

You'd think my immense attraction to this man would have, I don't know, chilled out since we started living together full time six months ago. But these ovaries say, *Chilled out? Chilled out, who?* So, here I am, still getting hot and bothered when Connor so much as breathes in my direction.

"Well, Wolfie and Pen can decide if it's worth fixing that when they arrive." Connor checks his watch, and I just enjoy the sight of him, still amazed that he can make noting the time look sexy. "By the way, did she text you an ETA?"

"Yup," I murmur, centering a hand on his chest as I lean into his broad frame to kiss him on the cheek. I can't help myself anymore. Just a taste before date night really gets going. "They should be here any second."

"Not soon enough."

He growls, dipping his head down to kiss me hungrily on the neck. My giggles are embarrassingly explosive.

Connor catches my lips in a slow, easy kiss—the kind of kiss I could easily lose hours of my life to. And even though all of my nerve endings are lit up like Christmas lights, the clock is ticking and date night hasn't even begun yet, so I pull back—but not before kissing him with everything I've got.

Without another word, he takes over baby supervision so I can scamper off to the bathroom and put some finishing touches on my makeup.

It's kind of impressive how we can so easily pass the guardian baton between us now, sharing so many months of caretaking together. Marley isn't my daughter, but that doesn't matter. Connor makes sure of it. We're a family now.

A favorite memory floats to the forefront of my mind. A glowing fireplace and several picture books strewn across my lap . . . Marley asleep in my arms and Connor dozing on my shoulder. It was that moment that I realized I don't have to be Marley's mom. I can just be Jessa, because Jessa belongs here.

It helps that Connor has this innate ability to sense when I need a moment to myself. And I certainly appreciate the few extra minutes in front of the mirror. We haven't gone out on a date in . . . I don't even want to count the months. Putting a number on it would force far too much pressure on this evening to be perfect. But that doesn't mean I won't try to make it the best night we've had in a while.

I'm not a stylist, by any means, but I know my way around some bronzer and a little eyeshadow. And let me tell you—this look? Smoky, warm, and all kinds of sexy. It's too bad this velvet slip dress will spend most of the night hidden away under a winter jacket . . . but such is early spring in Chicago, I'm learning. It's not *not* winter until it's very suddenly summer.

I'm just about done perfecting my lip liner when a knock echoes down the hall.

"They're here," I call, peeking my head out the bathroom door.

"I've got it," Connor calls back.

It occurs to me that we've still got all of our holiday decor up, even though we've long since entered Valentine's Day territory. It would be easy to kick myself for not cleaning up before having friends over, but a little voice in my head reminds me that I'm juggling a full-time job with co-parenting a tiny human—who isn't even a full year old yet, I might add.

I listen to the familiar voices of our friends at the door—Penelope's excited chirp, Wolfie's rumbling growl. Part of me wants to just cancel our plans and hang out with them, but we rarely get an opportunity like tonight for just the two of us. And I can't pass that up.

When I emerge from the bathroom, Penelope has a very pleased Marley propped on her hip.

"Oof, Marley girl. You're getting heavy."

"Milk o'clock is her favorite time of the day," I say with a shrug before pulling Penelope into a side hug and shooting a smile Wolfie's way, who returns it with a silent nod.

"You look so hot." Penelope gasps, making a show of looking me up and down before glaring at her brother with an adorable pout. "Hey, why do you always get to go on dates with Jessa? When's my turn?"

"*Always* is a strong word." Connor chuckles, but his voice is strained. Date night has historically come second to parenting, a pattern we're both guilty of falling into over the winter.

"How's work, Jessa?"

This earnest question comes from Wolfie, catching me a little off guard.

"Oh. It's great. We just finished processing a ton of citizenship paperwork, and one of the students I'm tutoring learned how to spell his name and all of his siblings' names this week. It's a lot of work, but it's very fulfilling."

I'm still not used to talking about my job. I mean, going from part-time nanny to full-time nonprofit employee is a pretty wild evolution. How much information do I share? How much do people care? I could go on and on, but I'm always careful not to bore people either.

"Sounds like good, decent work," Wolfie says with a serious expression. "Helping those in need through a substantial life change is no joke. You're better than the rest of us, that's for sure."

Not only have I never heard the man string so many words together in succession, but I've also never been so speechless. Before I try and fail to find the right response, Connor comes to my rescue. *Thank God.*

"That's not news to me." He chuckles, putting an arm around my shoulder and planting a warm kiss to my temple. "She works harder than anyone I've ever known. I'm lucky to be on her arm tonight."

I beam up at him. "Oh, stop . . ."

"It's true. I don't know how you do it. You deserve a break."

"And you deserve one too," Penelope says, raising an eyebrow at her brother in a look that says *we've had this conversation before.*

I reluctantly duck out from under Connor's arm to untangle Marley's chubby fingers from Penelope's hair. "We're so grateful to you both for coming out to watch her for a bit."

"Of course. I think the two of you taking a night to yourselves is a great idea. And I love spending time with my perfect, darling niece."

"And she loves spending time with your perfect, darling hair. Let up, Marley," I say, scolding her gently, but Penelope just laughs.

"C'mere, Wolfie. Hold her," Penelope says, and Connor and I share a look of mild alarm.

Has Wolfie ever held Marley? Has Wolfie ever held a child, period?

I watch in awe as Penelope passes Marley off to the gentle giant, who nestles the baby girl comfortably into his arm, keeping her head supported and her attention engaged. Penelope sighs happily, leaning against his bicep as they each offer a finger to Marley's eager hands.

"What do you think? Do you want one of these?" she teases, but I can hear the genuine curiosity in her voice.

I've never thought of Wolfie as a dad, but it kind of makes sense. The protectiveness, the no-nonsense attitude, the tenderness beneath all that rough exterior . . . He'd be a wonderful dad.

"I'm open to it."

The hint of a smile on Wolfie's lips mirrors Penelope's full-blown grin. Their happiness is contagious, and soon we're all grinning like the cast of a Hallmark movie, old holiday decor on the walls and all.

"Ready?" Connor squeezes my hand, and my heart says *bah-thump* loudly in my chest.

"Yeah, but . . . are you sure about this?" The question catapults out of my mouth despite my best intentions.

Connor sighs wearily, the hard line of his lips telling me he's in the exact same boat. The worry boat. We haven't left Marley in the care of friends for more than an hour before. There's really no knowing what to expect.

"It's not like I asked Caleb to watch her," Connor mumbles with a half smirk, his eyes twinkling with humor.

"Okay, true . . ."

"We have the guide you sent us, Jess," Penelope says with a reassuring smile. "We'll take good care of her."

Connor quirks an eyebrow at me. "Guide?"

I shrug sheepishly. "Yeah, just the basics. Bottle temperature, diaper protocol . . . you know."

"She typed it all up in a Word document," Penelope says with a grin.

Connor just smiles and pulls me into a tight hug. "How about we get going then?"

"Yes. Go, go."

Penelope shoos us down the hall, where Connor helps me into my coat and slides his arms into his own. After promising her that we won't be back until ten p.m. at the *earliest*, Connor and I are out the door and cruising down Lakeshore Drive in no time.

Car rides have always been a time for thinking, and this one's no exception. With my fingers intertwined with Connor's, my eyes glaze over as we thread through the nighttime tapestry of streetlamps and headlights.

It's wild how half a year can pass in the blink of an eye and sweep up everything that was once so true for me, replacing it with a whole new perspective on life. I went from nomad nanny with lofty ideals of saving the world to busy career woman with a tangible mission *and* dirty diapers to boot in barely any time at all.

As for creating a home with Connor? Well, it's been nothing short of a dream. He's so kind and thoughtful, and a freaking king in the sack. Living with him is like rooming with my best friend, my teammate, and my lover—all in one. I wouldn't trade it for the world.

Connor squeezes my hand. "What are you thinking about?"

"Hmm. I guess I'm thinking about how crazy it is that we met."

"Crazy how?"

"I mean, did you expect to find your child's nanny in the upstairs apartment of your neighbor's house? Or did you and the Wilkeses have a secret you aren't telling me?"

"No," he says with a chuckle. "I promise I wasn't part of the screening process. I didn't see you coming at all."

"Oh?"

"Nope. And I certainly didn't expect to fall in love with you."

"Oh, psh. You're telling me that the desperate dad in you didn't fall in love with the nanny on sight that day? That sweaty, red-faced Jessa didn't steal his heart?"

"Oh, she did." Connor]draws my knuckles to his lips to brush soft kisses against them. "He just didn't want to admit it yet."

"Well . . ." I sigh happily, looking out the window. "I'm glad we're us now."

"What do you mean?"

"Not the desperate dad. Not the hot mess of a nanny. *Us*."

"A unit," he says. "A team."

"A partnership."

"A comedy duo."

I laugh. "Is this a new game? How many ways can we say *we're together*?"

"Oh, I've got more if you do."

The rest of the car ride is a pleasant back-and-forth of jokes and general silliness. When we arrive at our dinner destination, I'm still recovering from his latest one-liner when I look out the window and catch sight of the green neon sign.

I gasp, my hand flying over my heart on instinct. "It's the bistro."

"Yeah," Connor says, his winning smile giving me all kinds of goose bumps. "I figured . . . we don't get a lot of time off. We could try something new, risk a little disappointment, or we could do something we've done before, because we know we like it."

"We do like it," I say, drooling at the memory of the delicious casserole we ordered last time. "And we know the wine is affordable."

"Right. So, that sounds like a yes to me."

Connor pulls the car around the block and grabs a ticket at the entrance to the dimly lit parking garage, an unspoken promise that we'll be taking our time tonight at the familiar bistro. When we park, I turn to Connor with an honest question.

"Does this make us boring old people?"

Connor laughs, and the sound is so wonderful that I find myself unbuckling my seat belt so I can lean across the car console and press an adoring kiss to his full, smiling lips. He sighs against my mouth, threading his fingers through the hair at the back of my neck to prolong the moment.

"I guess I don't mind being boring with you," I whisper breathlessly the moment our lips part. "And this time, I brought a coat."

"Why does that matter?"

"Because there are no cheeky sex seminars to

attend after we're done with dinner and tipsy on merlot," I sing in my best sultry voice, waggling my eyebrows and walking my fingers up his chest with each word. "So we're gonna walk to the lake."

"Yes, ma'am." Connor chuckles, guiding his thumb down my cheek to caress my lower lip. "But let's make one thing clear before we head in."

"What's that?"

Connor pulls me into him by the coat lapels, capturing my lips in a steamy, spine-tingling kiss that leaves me panting for more . . . for absolutely all of him. And when his kisses wander from my mouth to my cheek to the sensual line of my neck, I know for a fact dinner will be delayed.

"Life with you, Jessa McClaine, will never be boring."

Epilogue

CONNOR

The candle-lit hallway just outside of the reception hall is oddly comforting at a moment like this. Inside buzzes the chatter of dozens of guests. Inside promises hours upon hours of what is required to be one of the most memorable evenings of our lives. But inside also lies a whole lot of pressure.

But outside, with Jessa nestled deeply into my arms, is comfort. Serenity. She plays with the thick platinum band on my knuckle, the very ring she slid onto my finger not an hour ago, witnessed by all of our friends and family.

I pull her hand to my lips, brushing them against the jeweled engagement ring and a thinner, daintier band of her own. It's a stolen moment, one that will surely end as soon as the wedding party finds us.

With the ceremony done and pictures taken, it's all I can do not to whisk Jessa back home for our first night together as newlyweds.

But that will come later. First, we have to get through the reception.

"Are you ready?" she murmurs, tipping her chin to look up at me.

God, she's so beautiful, her makeup natural and simple, with only a bit of blush to accent her already rosy cheeks. I graze my fingertips across her temple, careful not to undo the hard work of the hair stylist who finessed all of Jessa's thick, unruly hair into an intricate knot of curls at the nape of her neck.

"Ready as I'll ever be," I whisper, kissing her forehead with a tenderness I reserve for the two most important girls in my life—this incomparable woman in my arms, and the little cherub just inside those doors, currently being cared for by her mom. My heart is filled to the brim with gratitude to whatever higher power decided to make me so damn lucky.

Soon, voices echo down the hall, and I give Jessa a squeeze. And just like that, it's time.

Our wedding party reappears, consisting of the men of Frisky Business, Penelope, and two of Jessa's friends from college. I would bet money that Maren and Scarlett have already made themselves and many other guests comfortable at the tables or the bar as our wedding-planner power duo.

Someone cues the DJ and the music begins, ushering in the whole party, pair by pair until it's just Jessa and me stepping over the threshold. The guests clap and cheer when I twirl her around, her lacy white gown billowing out around her. The introductions pass in a blur of toasts and speeches, either sweet and silly, depending on the speaker. Of course, the buffet is a hit, but not nearly as much as the open bar turns out to be.

Caleb jogs by me with two old fashioneds in his hands, a conspicuous bottle of wine in his suit pocket, and a wide-eyed expression on his face.

"I'm gathering rations for the rest," he says, panting as he gestures with an elbow to the corner of the room where the rest of the Frisky Business family has wandered. "Did you know the bar closes at ten? Gotta get 'em while they last."

"Yes, I know the bar closes at ten. I helped plan this wedding," I call after him, but he's already gone.

I watch my friends welcome him back with light applause as he distributes the drinks around the circle. The men lift their old fashioneds while Penelope, Maren, and Scarlett pop open another bottle of stolen wine. The sight of these familiar faces, flushed with the warmth and happiness of mutual celebration, fills me with a deep satisfaction.

Watching my friends, I'm considering giving up on my rotation of greetings and well wishes and instead spending the rest of the night with my preferred crowd. But not until I can locate Jessa and steal her away from chatty uncles and awkward colleagues.

Just then, a hand snakes around my waist. *Speak of the angel herself.*

"Hey, mister, got a minute?"

I grin, lacing fingers with my wife's. *My wife.*

"I think we've determined that you can have all my minutes from here on out."

"Hmm." She hums contentedly, leaning her head against my bicep. "Will you come with me to spend a little time with your daughter? She's getting grumpy, and I think Beth is going to take her home before it gets to be too late."

"Fair enough."

Marley's biological mom, Beth, and Jessa have

become close since she moved in with me. There's some sort of understanding between them that goes beyond the fun they have teasing me for my little fatherhood blunders. It's the connection between two compassionate humans who see a lot of themselves in each other.

"Da-da," Marley cries, squirming in Beth's arms when she catches sight of me.

Beth rolls her eyes with a smirk, passing our daughter off to me. "She's downright sick of me now, I'll tell you that much."

While Jessa laughingly consoles Beth, I spin my baby girl around, earning about a million giggles. Her curly hair is pulled into two tiny pigtails, and while she's still not great at walking, she's already such a strong and healthy child. It's uncommon to have one's child present on your wedding day, so I don't take the privilege lightly. I nuzzle my nose into her cheek, eliciting another bout of shrieking laughter.

"I love you so much, Marley girl," I whisper against her soft hair. "More than you'll ever know."

About ten minutes later, Beth leaves with Marley, and before long, the lights dim and the dancing begins.

Jessa dances with her stepdad, who keeps her

laughing from pretty much the first step until the last. I dance with my mother, who spends the brief five minutes worrying about when Penelope will get married to that nice, stoic man she's been carting around to family gatherings lately.

Our own slow dance goes off without a hitch, despite my stumbling feet betraying me at the rehearsal. I'm pretty damn sure the only reason I don't make a complete ass of myself is just because I'm so distracted by the exquisite woman in my arms, who whispers the steps to me between reassuring kisses.

It wasn't rehearsed, but Jessa doesn't mind one bit when I dip her at the end of the song, pressing a less than family-friendly kiss to her neck in front of God and all our guests. The guys are a few drinks in by this time, their hooting and hollering inspiring a loud reaction from the crowd.

Finally, it's time for the bouquet toss.

Jessa pretends to line up her shot before spinning around and tossing the flowers wildly over her head. Much to my shock, it's Scarlett who catches the damn thing, staring at it like she's caught a live grenade. Maren and Penelope cheer, wrapping their arms around the reluctant winner and squeezing her tight.

Meanwhile, my focus is on Hayes, Wolfie, and Caleb from their seats at a nearby table. Maybe it's the lighting playing tricks on me, but I don't think I've ever seen Caleb so pale in his life.

"I've always wanted to do that," Jessa says, running full tilt into my arms.

I hug her tight, lifting her slightly so her feet dangle in the air for a second.

She groans happily. "Oh, that's nice. These shoes are trying to kill me."

"How about I give you a nice, long foot rub in the tub when we finally make it home tonight?" I murmur into her ear, letting my lips tickle her skin. "I'll snag some of that leftover cake, and we can finally drink that bubbly we've been saving in the fridge."

Jessa pulls back, just far enough to kiss me hard on the lips. "Marry me."

"Done."

"I love you." Her grin is as infectious as it is lovable.

And I'm as lucky as I am smitten. "I love you too."

Later, after many dances, well wishes from relatives, and even more stolen kisses with my new bride, guests slowly trickle out of the exits toward their cars and Ubers. The staff makes quick work of the mess. The lights, the decorations, even the tiny little placards for name inserts all get packed away into boxes for another night, another wedding. Jessa hugs Penelope, Maren, and Scarlett good night while I shake the hands of my business partners and friends.

Something still seems off about Caleb, so I clasp his hand and pull him in for a bro hug.

"Do you have a sec?" he asks when I pull back to clap him on the shoulder. "To talk."

I glance at Jessa, who catches my eye and reads my mind instantly. She shoots me a wink as if to say *good luck* before turning back to her friends.

"Yeah, man, what's up?"

"I don't even know where to start. It's about Scarlett."

Okay. Unexpected plot twist, but I roll with it, giving him a nod. "Of course."

He gestures me over to a terrace that's semi-private, and we step out onto it.

"So, what's going on?" I meet his eyes, trying to rack my brain and think if I've seen anything unusual going on between them. I haven't. Though I guess I've been pretty wrapped up in my own stuff lately, so I really haven't been paying attention.

With a deep sigh, he runs one hand through his rumpled hair. Then he begins.

I listen as Caleb fills me in on his sudden and growing feelings for his friend Scarlett. Honestly, it's all so unexpected, for a moment I'm speechless.

"Say something, dude," he grumbles, clearly annoyed with me.

"Sorry." I raise one hand. "I'm just processing."

Jessa chooses that moment to appear beside us and grins when she sees me. "There you are."

I lean over to give her cheek a kiss. "Sorry I disappeared. We're just talking for a second."

She looks between Caleb and me, her brow crinkling. "Everything okay?"

I nod. "Just some guy talk."

Caleb clears his throat. "You might as well tell her. I'm sure you will anyway."

I chuckle. "You sure?"

He shrugs. "You're married now. I basically think of you guys as one person anyway."

This pulls an uneasy laugh out of Jessa. "Okay, now you're worrying me. Is something wrong?"

Caleb shakes his head. "No, nothing's wrong."

I take her hand, smoothing my thumb over her knuckles. "Caleb was just confiding in me about his feelings . . . for someone."

"Scarlett," Jessa says with a smile.

"How did you know?" Caleb asks, his voice slightly strained. "Was I that obvious?"

"No," I say at the same time that Jessa answers, "Yes."

We all chuckle, and Caleb shakes his head.

"I noticed you being a little extra . . . attentive toward her. That's all," Jessa says with a wave.

"And do you think Scar would . . ." Caleb runs one hand over the back of his neck.

"Be down with that scenario?" Jessa asks. "Heck yes, I do. I think she feels all kinds of things for you too that blur the friend zone."

Caleb's answering grin is huge.

I clap one hand on his shoulder. "Listen, buddy, as much as we'd love to stand out here all night and dole out relationship advice, we've kinda got a wedding night to look forward to."

He nods solemnly. "I hear ya. You two kids go have fun. Go make Marley a baby brother or sister."

Jessa laughs. "No way. Not yet anyhow. Work is crazy right now, and she's still so young."

I take her hand, nodding. "We have time."

It's one of the first conversations Jessa and I had when she moved in—about our future and what we both wanted. More kids was one of the things on both of our lists. But we both decided there was no rush, and we would take our time over the course of several years.

"So, should I go talk to her?" Caleb asks.

"Yes," both Jessa and I say at the same time, laughing.

Caleb shakes his head and heads toward the ballroom. "Okay, but if this blows up in my face, I'm holding you two accountable," he calls over one shoulder.

"It won't," Jessa calls back.

I pull her into my arms and sway with her as we watch him go, cautiously approaching Scarlett.

"You sure about that?" I tip my chin toward Caleb and Scarlett.

She shrugs. "Not entirely. But he won't know until he tries."

It makes me think about if I'd never told Jessa how I felt. My life would be sad and cold and empty. She brightens my days and my nights with her infectious laughter and tender love. I couldn't be more grateful for this woman by my side.

"Should we get out of here?" I ask.

"Thought you'd never ask," she murmurs, turning in my arms to give me a big hug.

I lean into Jessa's embrace, so thankful for everything life has given me—great friendships, a successful business, a sweet daughter, and a beautiful wife who I vow silently in this moment to love forever and ever.

Amen.

I hope you enjoyed Connor and Jessa's story. Up next is the first in a brand new hockey series, *The Rebel*.

Turn the page for a sneak preview.

THE
REBEL

ONE

Eden

"**D**on't look now," my best friend, Gretchen, says with a knowing smirk. "Here comes trouble."

Didn't I know it?

Alex Braun was six feet of hockey god with a side of naughty trouble. Problem was, I liked being a little naughty. When it came to him, anyway. What good girl didn't have a little streak of bad inside them?

But one stolen, *perfect* kiss aside, I still wasn't sure Alex actually even knew who I was.

And who am I these days?

In high school, I was the governor's daughter.

The first daughter of a wealthy conservative family, I was smart and driven and unflinching in my beliefs.

Now, though? Three years in at Sutton, the small Boston university that has become my new home . . . I'm changing, and so is my family.

My dad is no longer governor. No, that ended horribly with a scandal involving his secretary, and my parents are no longer married. And me? Well, the itch to do something reckless is right there, clawing at me from just below the surface. I want to do something that's for me and me alone.

And Alex Braun is at the very top of that to-do list.

Gretchen knows this, which is why she's currently elbowing me in the ribs as Alex steps into the crowded living room.

The parties on frat row generally aren't our thing, but the hockey team won their game tonight, which meant they'd be out celebrating. Which meant the chances of running into Alex again were excellent. So I dressed in a pair of tight jeans and a cute black top, curled my hair, and dragged Gretchen out with me.

Alex lifts the cup to his mouth again, taking a long drink. One of his teammates practically mauls him, and Alex's perfect mouth breaks into a happy smile.

I'm transfixed by his chiseled jaw. Straight white teeth. Messy dark blond hair. Mischievous nature.

"Tonight's the night," Gretchen says, and I nod.

"Yeah," I mumble, momentarily struck inarticulate. The nerves swimming inside my belly are part excitement and part fear. The fear of rejection is strong, rearing its ugly head whenever I imagine going up to Alex and telling him what I want.

And what I want is *him*.

Our kiss last weekend at a party similar to this one has replayed through my head all week. Alex is responsible for a lot of crushes all over campus, but I felt something that night, a spark between us. For one brief, shining moment, his eyes met mine, and I was no longer the boring coed with straight As and too many responsibilities. I was someone fun and daring and desirable.

For him, it was nothing more than some stupid dare, but for me, it was much, much more. Goose bumps raised along my skin, and my heart pounded out an uneven rhythm.

Alex's mouth was shockingly erotic, hot and

commanding, and my knees literally trembled. I reached out, pressing one hand into his firm shoulder for balance, needing the support if I had any hope of remaining upright. His tongue touched mine in confident, measured strokes, and I let out a little hum of satisfaction.

Which is really no surprise. Alex has a certain reputation on the hockey team. The guy can score. His room practically has a revolving door of gorgeous girls all looking for one thing—a hot night of fun. And I'm not ashamed to admit that I'm no different.

Over the past week, I've done some digging and learned that Alex is on a full athletic scholarship for hockey, that he's a top recruit and is expected to go to the NHL draft next year instead of finishing his senior year at Sutton.

Which means I need to make my move quickly, before he moves on.

Plus, I'm not the type of girl to sit around and wait for things to happen. I'm more of a grab-life-by-the-balls type. At least, I am lately. After my dad's fiasco, I learned that nothing lasts forever, and it's best to take what you can, when you can.

But my window of opportunity is shrinking right before my eyes.

Gretchen and I watch as a perky blond member of Kappa Nu approaches Alex. He smiles at her as she speaks, his gaze lowering from her lips to her ample breasts. Her mouth twists into a smile, and then she takes one of his big calloused hands and tugs, leading him across the living room and right up the stairs. And Alex follows like a puppy.

My stomach drops to my knees.

Gretchen meets my eyes with a worried look. "Shit."

I shrug, trying not to let her see my disappointment. "It's fine," I lie.

It's irrational, but the flare of rejection stings. Coupled with my family's fall from grace and the high expectations for me to succeed, it's too much.

I've imagined Alex and me as a power couple. Him the athletic sports star with the big smile and fun-loving attitude, and me with the brains and drive and connections. He'd see what a perfect match we'd make and abandon his fuck-boy ways. Every guy's gotta grow up sometime, right? And if Eden Wynn isn't the kind of girl you settle down with, then who the hell is?

My mantra is in my last name—Wynn at all costs. It's what I do.

Gretchen is still watching me with a worried look.

"I'll be right back. I'm going to find something different to drink." My voice comes out steady, but inside, I feel anything but. I feel like I'm spinning out of control—like I'm on one of those tilt-a-wheel rides at the carnival.

Gretchen's expression darkens but she nods. I'm not quite sure she believes me, but I don't care.

Hurrying, I make it up the stairs in time to see Alex and the girl disappear into a bedroom. My heart hammers out a painful rhythm. This isn't how I wanted tonight to go.

The door doesn't close all the way like I expect it to, and my feet stop moving, stuck here in the center of the hallway. I don't dare move because I'm certain the creaky wooden floorboards will give me away. The music from downstairs is only a distant thumping sound up here, which means I can hear the faint rustling of clothes.

"Jesus," Alex grunts.

I hate myself for it a little, but I dare to take one cautious step closer, then another, until I can see through the crack in the door.

The sight isn't one I expected. I thought there

would be a passionate display of groping each other, arms wrapped around bodies, and kisses so hot you could feel them deep down in your soul. That's the kind of kisses I've fantasized about sharing with him all week long.

Instead, Alex stands like a statue carved from stone, muscular and unmoving except for his chest, which hitches with quick, shallow breaths. His gaze is downcast, —captured by the girl perched on her knees between his parted feet. Her hands work furiously at undoing his belt buckle. I hear the clank of metal, and my heart squeezes.

I can't see it from this vantage point, but it's obvious the second she gets his cock free. Because her head bobs, and he releases a strangled sound.

"*Fuck.*" He groans, squeezing his eyes closed and fisting her hair.

I force a breath into my lungs and stagger one step back.

"Spying?"

The deep rasp of a masculine voice startles me and I whirl around, my heart in my throat.

"No." The word leaves my mouth at the same moment I register who's joined me in the hallway.

Holt Rossi.

If Alex is the golden jock, then Holt is the brooding loner. He's imposing and powerful, and standing here before him, I feel a little unsteady. He's huge, with a broad chest. Wide shoulders. Chiseled jaw. And he looks ticked off.

"I was looking for something else to drink. The beer is awful." It's not a complete lie.

He nods. "Come on."

For reasons unknown, I follow him down the hall. Maybe it's because he believes my lie. Maybe it's because I *really* don't want to listen to my crush getting a blow job.

Holt and I had English composition together freshman year, and two classes together sophomore year. In one of them, we were assigned partners for a semester-long project. Then he declared his major—criminal justice—and our shared classes stopped. This year I've only seen him a handful of times. His hair is longer, and he looks like he forgot how to shave, but his eyes are still the same dark gray, expressive with a hidden depth I've never quite understood.

He unlocks a door, and I follow him inside.

It takes me a minute to realize we're inside his bedroom. It's a small room in what appears to be a converted attic, with wood-paneled walls and a sloping ceiling that makes him duck as we enter.

"You live here?"

He nods. "Moved in last semester. Free rent."

"Why would Theta give you free rent?"

I know he's not in the fraternity. I'm pretty sure he's against what all fraternities stand for—fun, camaraderie, and brotherhood. Holt Rossi doesn't like relying on anyone but himself.

"Because I tutor the underclassmen, and I also do all the grounds maintenance. Lawn care, snow removal, et cetera."

I nod. "Gotcha."

Holt grabs a silver flask from his dresser and holds it out to me.

I certainly don't want whatever mystery liquor is inside. I've never been a big drinker, but since I lied and told him I was up here searching for something to drink, I don't want to blow my cover.

I accept the flask and take a small sip. It's surprisingly smooth, but the burn of whiskey lingers on my tongue.

When I pass the flask back to him, Holt brings it to his mouth, placing his lips where mine were a second ago as he takes a long pull. The thought of it sends a small flash of something foreign racing through me, and I look away.

His bedroom is sparely decorated with a twin-size bed on a metal frame, no headboard, and a single pillow. I sleep with at least six pillows. Excessive? Yes, but I like what I like.

His dresser is tall and narrow. One of the drawers sags like it's been pulled from its frame and never quite settled back in the same way again. A desk sits under the small round window, piled under the weight of textbooks and an ancient-looking laptop.

For the first time, I wonder about Holt, about his history, about what kind of things he likes to do, what type of girls he dates.

If I'm the well-bred society type that people assume me to be, then Holt Rossi is the opposite. From a working-class family, and here on a merit scholarship.

It's only natural that I should wonder about him. Right?

"You're not his type." Holt's deep voice pulls me from my thoughts again.

"Huh?"

"Braun."

I lift one shoulder, trying to look disinterested, but his words slice straight through me, stealing the air from my lungs for a moment.

When Holt passes me the flask again, this time I accept it eagerly, grateful for the distraction. I take a longer sip, letting the whiskey warm a path inside me.

"Why wouldn't I be his type?" I wipe my mouth with the back of my hand.

"Because." Holt shrugs, taking the flask back and draining it. "You're a good girl. You give off girlfriend vibes. And I'm pretty sure Braun is allergic to monogamy."

His words sting, but maybe . . . somewhere deep inside, they make sense. If it's true that Alex will be entering the NHL draft next year, why would he want to be saddled with a college girlfriend?

Holt pulls out the chair that's tucked neatly into the space in front of the desk and offers it to me. I lower myself onto it while he takes a seat on the end of his bed.

Whereas Alex is athletically handsome in a rugged, hockey player kind of way with his thick thighs, bulky forearms, and messy hair, Holt gives off a hot bad boy vibe. He's tall, even bigger than Alex, and judging by the rough stubble on his jaw, his face hasn't seen a razor in weeks. But his eyes are kind, warm like melted honey. I've always liked his eyes.

"It doesn't matter," I say at last, realizing Holt's still watching me like a butterfly captured in a net. "It won't be happening. Not now." I look across the room to the door where only a few paces away, Alex Braun is probably fucking some poor girl's throat.

Holt's tone softens. "He doesn't deserve it, you know that, right?"

I can't figure out how he's so perceptive. How he seems to know what I've been planning with Alex tonight. Not that I'd ever admit it to him.

"*It?*" It is a crass way to refer to someone's virginity, and my tone more than hints at my annoyance.

"Your *devotion*," Holt says to clarify, one dark eyebrow raised in my direction.

I straighten my shoulders. "Oh. Right."

Holt clears his throat and looks away. I'm not sure if he's embarrassed for me or simply giving me a moment. I release a slow exhale and try to collect myself. My hands are still shaking.

"You have any more of that?" I tip my chin toward the flask on his dresser.

Holt's mouth lifts in a crooked smirk, and I think it's probably the closest to an actual smile I've ever seen from him. He doesn't give off any warm and fuzzy vibes, but at the same time, I feel safe with him.

I recall sophomore year after studying together in the library, he insisted on walking me back to my dorm after we realized it had gotten dark outside. He waited on the stoop, even though it was raining and he was without an umbrella, as I unlocked the door. He didn't move from that spot until I waved at him from my second story window. Then he'd tipped his chin down and shouldered his heavy backpack and stalked away.

"Sure." He rises from the bed and opens the top dresser drawer, producing the bottle from which I assume the flask was filled.

When he hands it to me, I twist off the cap and take a sip. I can already feel myself growing warm and slightly tipsy.

"So, what's your story?" I ask.

"My story?"

I shrug. "Your major. Life plans . . . you know."

I already know his major, but I don't want to

seem like a creeper. I also know he works part time as a bouncer at the off-campus bar called the Tavern, a regular weekend hotspot. He checks IDs at the door and breaks up fights when things occasionally get too rowdy.

Holt shifts his weight. "There's not much to tell. I grew up in a small town in New Jersey, a few hours outside of New York. And I got out as soon as I could."

"Family?"

He makes an annoyed sound. "I guess you could call them that. No one I'm close with."

I nod once. Despite the image the Wynns like to give off, I know what it's like to come from a dysfunctional family. "My home life was tough too. Probably not like yours, but still . . . tough."

Holt doesn't shrug or laugh off my discomfort when I say this. I'm certain he knows I come from money, and that my dad was the governor, so he could. He could pat me on the head and patronize me about my little privileged life.

Instead, he meets my eyes with a look of understanding. Not sympathy, not pity, but something like understanding. On some level, we're sharing our secrets, and it's more than I've done with anyone in three years at this school. Even with Gretchen.

Holt's attention is yanked away by a scuffle in the hall and loud voices. I turn my head toward the door, listening, wondering if one of them is Alex's. Wondering if it's time to go. Then there's a dull thud of someone being shoved into the wall and the sound of furniture scraping across the floor.

"Stay here," Holt says as he goes off to investigate, leaving me alone in his bedroom.

Loud footsteps thump down the stairs, and I cross the room. When I peek into the hall, it's quiet and empty. The voices are downstairs now, angry male shouts, though I can't make out what they're saying.

The door to the room Alex was in opens, and I quickly shut Holt's door, tucking myself inside once again. The girl he was with says something and he laughs, then there are two sets of footsteps as they descend the stairs together.

I pull out my phone and see a text from Gretchen.

Where are you???

        Upstairs, I reply with shaking hands.

I have no idea why I still feel nervous. On edge. Maybe it's because I was almost caught for a second time by Alex?

But I know that's not it. It's because I've been basically hiding up here with Holt.

A reply comes from Gretchen.

There's a fight outside. I'm leaving. You okay or do you need a ride?

Alex and his flavor of the night are gone. So, why am I still hiding out in Holt's bedroom?

Making up my mind, I text a response.

I'll be okay.

Suit yourself! **Gretchen types back.** Let me know if you change your mind and I'll come get you.

I text her back the thumbs-up emoji.

Holt still hasn't returned, so I pocket my cell phone and cross the room to his little wooden desk that sits under the window. There's a notebook on top, and when I flip it open, I scan the page, trying to understand what I'm reading.

I'D HAD ENOUGH OF THE MINDLESS GAMES

THEN YOU APPEARED

WITH EYES SO BLUE AND HAIR SO SOFT

I'LL NEVER BE THE SAME

Song lyrics? Poetry? I'm not sure, but I don't want to snoop. The sound of approaching footsteps pulls me away from the desk and whatever private thoughts are hidden away in Holt's journal.

Holt bursts into the room, breathing hard. He's holding his fist near his side, and his normally stoic expression is twisted into a scowl.

"Fucking frat boys," he mutters under his breath as I cross the room to him.

"What happened?"

He doesn't answer. Instead, he swallows hard, looking pissed off.

"You're bleeding," I say, appraising him with concern.

His knuckles are scraped, and there's a drop of blood on the corner of his lower lip.

"I'm fine, Eden. You should probably go."

Holt's tone is flat, and he won't meet my eyes.

"I'm not leaving you like this."

I touch the pad of my finger to his lip. I have no idea why I do it . . . I've never touched him before. Maybe it's because I've never noticed his mouth before. His lips are full and soft, and I don't like the sight of blood on his mouth.

When he speaks again, his voice is softer. "Believe me, I'm fine."

I wave him toward the bed. "You're not fine. Sit down."

Acknowledgments

Thank you so much, lovely readers! You are the reason I get to continue bringing my stories to life, and I truly hope you enjoyed this series as much as I did. I'm starting a brand-new series and returning to the world of sports romance. I sincerely hope you'll take this journey with me. The series is called Looking to Score, and Book One is titled *The Rebel*.

A huge amount of gratitude is owed to my lovely assistant, Alyssa; to my editors Rachel and Pam; to my agent, Jane; and to my audio production team. You're all truly outstanding at what you do. And to my sweet little family . . . I couldn't do it without you.

Get Two Free Books

Sign up for my newsletter and I'll automatically
send you two free books.

www.kendallryanbooks.com/newsletter

Follow Kendall

Website

www.kendallryanbooks.com

Facebook

www.facebook.com/kendallryanbooks

Twitter

www.twitter.com/kendallryan1

Instagram

www.instagram.com/kendallryan1

Newsletter

www.kendallryanbooks.com/newsletter/

Other Books By Kendall Ryan

Unravel Me

Filthy Beautiful Lies Series

The Room Mate

The Play Mate

The House Mate

Screwed

The Fix Up

Dirty Little Secret

xo, Zach

Baby Daddy

Tempting Little Tease

Bro Code

Love Machine

Flirting with Forever

Dear Jane

Only for Tonight

Boyfriend for Hire

The Two-Week Arrangement

Seven Nights of Sin

Playing for Keeps

All the Way

Trying to Score

Crossing the Line

The Bedroom Experiment

Down and Dirty

Crossing the Line

Wild for You

Taking His Shot

How to Date a Younger Man

Penthouse Prince

The Boyfriend Effect

My Brother's Roommate

The Stud Next Door

For a complete list of Kendall's books, visit:

www.kendallryanbooks.com/all-books/